Stormy Encounter

Love Rekindled in a Cabin

Zoe London

from various sources. Please consult a licensed professional before attempting any techniques outlined in this book.

By reading this document, the reader agrees that under no circumstances is the author responsible for any losses, direct or indirect, that are incurred as a result of the use of the information contained within this document, including, but not limited to, errors, omissions, or inaccuracies.

Table of Contents

Chapter 1

The mountains captivated Luna. She stared at the overwhelming beauty before her, glad she had decided to come along with her boss, Frank. He was a paunchy and slightly obese man, with a good sense of humor.

It was supposed to be a business trip, or so she had told her husband Marcus. But Luna knew it was the away time she so desperately wanted. The need had been gnawing away at her for quite some time now, but she had no idea where it had come from. On this trip into the Swiss mountains, she intended to find out.

Slightly weary after her trek through the snow, she halted to take a breather. Frank was at her side, wheezing slightly, obviously feeling his weight.

Luna sat down on an outcropping of rock, and Frank came and sat down beside her. Neither spoke. As Luna lifted her right hand and wiped her nose, an unknown smell from her arm triggered a sudden rush of memories.

She remembered her mother, and the rooms she'd lived in. Her mother Edna cleaned houses for a living and Luna had often gone along with her to help. She hated cleaning houses, but she loved her mother very much. And there had always been the mansion! She had loved to go there, not so much to do housework as to meet her friend Aiden.

He was a boy almost her own age, and he'd lived in the mansion. He came from a rich family and their friendship was a little unusual. She had never realized that, until the day her mother took her by the arm and told her the facts of life. Boys from wealthy families never married girls from poor families. Aiden would ultimately marry someone of his class. Luna smiled as she remembered her mother's words. At the time, she could not comprehend the reality her mother so clearly tried to show her. What had money to do with friendship? And Aiden wanted to be her friend. It was much later in life that she had finally understood. By then, their paths had taken different turns.

As the memories receded, Luna stood up and stretched her arms. She felt braced; the mountain air was cold and exhilarating. She stamped her foot a couple of times to get the circulation going. Turning to Frank, who was watching her in silence, she said, "I want to go up this slope a little more. Coming?"

Frank cast a speculative eye at the sky. "Looks like a bit of bad weather is coming our way. Let's go back. We can come back tomorrow."

Luna considered this for a few seconds. "I'm going to go up, to check out the view from the top of that slope," she said with determination.

Frank hesitated, he was unsure of what to do.

"You can go back to the village and wait for me, I won't be long. Meet you back at the restaurant. How's that?" said Luna, beginning to move up the slope. She was in good physical shape, slim and well-proportioned. She went to the gym often to keep her body in fighting condition.

"Right. But Luna, don't take any risks—the weather is beginning to close in," Frank warned, pointing upwards. Luna grinned and started briskly moving up the slope.

Frank began his journey back to the village with a slight feeling of unease. He knew that storms in the mountains were unlike anything at sea level. The weather was unpredictable and could turn nasty in seconds. Why wouldn't women see reason, for God's sake!

As he began walking down toward the village where they were staying, Frank pulled out his cell phone. There was a signal—weak, but present. He turned around toward where Luna was clambering up the slope in almost knee-deep snow.

"Make sure you have a signal on your phone!" he yelled.

Luna just waved her right arm in a dismissive gesture. Something was driving her to the top of the slope, and she had no time for warnings.

Frank gave up and started clumping back to his lodgings. The wind he noticed was stronger. He shook his head in frustration. He was worried about Luna.

By now, Luna was beginning to feel a little breathless, but she pressed on. The summit of the slope was within striking distance. Now was not the time to stop.

The snowfall had petered out, but the wind seemed to be increasing in strength. Luna pulled out her cell phone and looked at the screen. The signal was extremely poor, but at least it was there. Looking around her at the panorama that was visible, Luna saw white all around, broken with groves of trees with white tops. *They all have white hair,* thought Luna, *just like old men.*

She smiled to herself and tried to locate Gretchen, where she and Frank had rooms, but failed to find the village. Luna hugged herself. She was feeling a sense of freedom, which she hadn't experienced in a very long time. Looking around, she spotted a rock to sit on where she could still see the incredible view that lay all around her. It was at this point that her cell phone emitted a beep.

The sound broke her reverie. Her mind told her to ignore the call, but it might be Frank, or her husband. But when Luna glanced at the screen, she saw it was her mother calling. Luna sighed. This was a call she had to take, otherwise her mother would panic. She pressed the 'accept' button and put the device to her ear.

"Hello, Mom! How are you?"

"I hear that you're on another one of your business trips," came the plaintive voice of her mother, whom Luna knew didn't like when she traveled for work.

"Who told you that? Marcus?" Luna asked.

"Well, yes. He called to tell me that Sarah wanted to spend some time with me."

"What else did he tell you? Besides your granddaughter wanting to stay with you?"

Luna knew that her daughter, Susan, worshipped her grandmother.

"Nothing! Why, is there something he should have mentioned?" There was a pause, then her mother continued with a hint of anxiety in her voice, "Nothing wrong between the two of you, is there?"

"Mom, the signal here is very weak, and we may be cut off at any moment. Listen, there are no problems. Keep your granddaughter with you for a few days. She really loves you. I will be back in no time. Okay?" Luna spoke in a rush, eager to get off the phone.

"Yes, yes, that' s okay. God bless and bye," replied her mother, disconnecting the line.

Luna stared at the phone. Had she been too abrupt? Sighing, she put away the device. Had Marcus hinted at something? Or was her mother just guessing? Her mother could always sense trouble. Luna would call her back once she returned to Gretchen.

The wind had died down. Maybe the storm was passing her by.

But her memories were not.

The call from her mother had brought the memories back with a vengeance. Luna's mind drifted to her high school days, to her mother, and finally returned to Aiden. Images flooded her mind, a myriad of images. Luna closed her eyes in an effort to shut off the kaleidoscope of memories, but to no avail. She was back in the past.

The grounds of the mansion house were large and beautifully landscaped, surrounded by woods. Aiden was under the large fir tree, waiting for her. The housekeeping had taken longer than she had anticipated.

"You're late," Aiden pointed out with mock severity.

"Unlike you, I have to work for a living," she retorted.

Aiden just smiled. "Come on, let's go into the woods. I have some cookies."

Luna followed Aiden. She enjoyed these moments with him enormously, as they were often the only high point of her days. She loved the woods, and the wind that whispered through the green leaves and boughs. Walking by his side, she felt a sense of contentment. She knew she was a little boyish in her appearance, which was probably why the boys in her school didn't pay her much attention. But Aiden treated her like a lady. With him, she felt her femininity—she was a girl.

They arrived at the clearing and sat down. Aiden took out a paper packet and extracted two cookies. He handed one to Luna, telling her that they were homemade. As they munched the cookies, they looked at each other. Luna felt that Aiden was about to say something, but he kept his silence. She knew Aiden was attracted to her, but he was unable to admit it. She looked at his brown eyes and almost black curly hair. He was, thought Luna, an extremely handsome man.

As the image began to fade, Luna opened her eyes. Her spirits had improved considerably. But the sky was darker and the wind had started up again. The weather now looked threatening. She stood up and looked around to see the way back to Gretchen. Her footprints, however, had vanished. She looked around, a little bewildered.

From somewhere lower down, she heard the blare of sirens, along with a faint voice saying something. She strained to hear the announcement but the words were inaudible. And as she turned to move toward the sound of the voice, she noticed the clouds had quietly covered the sky, moving rapidly in the strengthening wind. The storm was about to begin.

She needed to start walking down. The announcement continued, but Luna was unable to figure out which direction it was coming from. It seemed to drift from left to right. Aiming for the midpoint, she slowly started down. The slope was a gentle gradient, not too steep, and Luna was able to walk without too much effort. It was the wind that was the problem. It was now blowing with increasing intensity, and unless she was careful, it would knock her down. She stumbled and felt a jolt of fear, cursing herself for not listening to Frank. The storm was slowly picking up speed, and visibility was getting worse. She held her left hand across her face to protect her eyes from the wind.

After a few steps, she stopped, pulled out her cell phone, and started to dial Frank's number before she realized there was no signal. She held the phone up and turned herself around to see if she could find enough of a signal to call Frank and ask for help. But she was out of luck. Try as she might, there was no service. She looked around for any markers to guide her way down but found nothing. She couldn't just stand there, though—she had to move quickly before she lost visibility altogether.

Recognizing that she was in a lot of trouble, she began blundering down, trusting the Almighty to guide her steps. As she crunched through the snow, she visualized the comfort of the hotel where she was staying. The log fire, the warmth, Frank sitting and talking… The vision faded as she suddenly felt herself moving downward—*falling* downward, she realized a split second later. She threw out her hands to stop the movement but it had no effect whatsoever. She slid down into a pit, hitting the bottom with a thud. For a few seconds, she just lay there, getting her bearings. Looking upward, she saw the sky. Slowly, she stood up and felt her legs and arms. She was unhurt.

At its broadest, the bottom of the pit was about three feet across. Luna stood for a minute, studying her predicament. She was down a hole and it was getting dark, with a storm coming on. The hole wasn't very deep; the edge was barely two feet above her outstretched hands. She tried to jump and reach the edge, without success. Her hands kept slipping on the snow. Hoping against hope that her cell phone would have a signal, even a weak one, she pulled it out of her jacket and looked at it. No signal. She held it up as close to the mouth of the hole as possible, but nothing seemed to work.

In desperation, she began calling for help. After a minute of panicked shouting, she stopped to take a breath. She had a feeling that this was the end of the line for her. She began to see visions of her childhood, her mother, and their house—until her visions were interrupted by a voice.

Chapter 2

Twenty-one years ago...

Edna Warren and her daughter Luna lived in a small two-room house in the Hudson Valley, where Edna worked as a housekeeper.

One morning, Edna was about to go to work when she saw her 11-year-old daughter walking home from school. Surprised, she stopped and waited for Luna to come closer.

"What's the matter? School let out early?" she asked.

Luna nodded.

"Was there some sort of problem, Luna, baby?"

"No, Mamma, no problem," said Luna.

"Are you sure about that?" Edna asked, studying her daughter's face closely. Seeing nothing untoward, she added, "Food is in the fridge. Warm it up; I have to go."

Luna watched her mother walk briskly away. Edna, despite being close to forty, was physically fit. She had to be; she needed to work, put food on the table. Her husband had deserted her when Luna was just five, just disappeared without warning. Edna had been a mother and a father figure for Luna ever since.

Luna heated her food and, finishing her meal, sat down to read. She loved books. Her reading was interrupted by a knock on the door. She walked up to the window by the door and peered out. A man was standing outside with his hands behind his back.

"Who is it?" she said.

The man looked around, seeming a little unsure as to where the words had come from. Then, noticing Luna at the window, he walked over.

"Is Mrs. Edna Warren at home?" he asked.

"No, she isn't. She has gone to work."

The stranger stood for a few seconds, as if undecided what to do.

"Well, will you please tell her that the Samuelsons want to know if she would be interested in taking up housekeeping at the mansion? You know the mansion, right?"

"Yes, I know the mansion," said Luna.

"If she's interested, tell her to be at the mansion in the morning. At about 11," said the man, and, waving his right hand in a gesture of farewell, he turned and walked off.

Luna went back to her book, but she was distracted. The mansion! It was a big house, with expansive grounds and trees. The place was beautiful to look at, and the Samuelsons were known to be extremely rich people. *They will pay well,* thought Luna.

When Edna returned from work, she found Luna asleep. She went about her work quietly. She did not want to wake Luna. Finishing her lunch she lay down to rest. Housekeeping she thought was back breaking work.

It was Luna who woke first. The sun was setting and the shadows of the trees were lengthening slowly. Rubbing her eyes, she walked to the bathroom to splash water on her face. Suddenly, she remembered the invitation to the mansion.

"Mamma, Mamma, wake up! I have good news for you!" she said, shaking her mother.

Edna awoke with a start. "What good news?" she mumbled, sounding groggy.

"The Samuelsons want you to work at the mansion!" Luna told her excitedly.

"The Samuelsons?" repeated Edna, looking curiously at her daughter.

"Yes, Mamma, they sent a man down earlier today. He wanted to meet you. When I told him you were away at work, he gave me the message," Luna explained.

"And what message was that?" Edna smiled.

"You are to go to the mansion at 11 tomorrow morning."

"I see," said Edna, getting up and sitting down on her favorite chair.

She closed her eyes and began to think. She thought about her future and Luna's. Where were their lives heading? Where would she be in another year from now? Would she have enough money to send her daughter to school? She sighed and decided to leave it to destiny, hoping it would be kinder in the future.

She made up her mind. She would finish one house first thing in the morning and then come home, change, and go to the mansion at 11. She would do the second house after the appointment at the mansion. If she got the job, she would serve notice to the Simpsons.

"What are you going to do, Mamma?"

"I will go to the mansion tomorrow and meet the owners. Let me see what they want me to do," said Edna, smiling at her daughter.

"But won't it be too much for you?" asked Luna. She didn't want her mother to work harder than she already did.

"I will have to give up the Simpsons," Edna explained.

"The Simpsons won't like it, Mamma!" Luna laughed.

She had accompanied her mother several times to the Simpson house, and she disliked Mrs. Simpson very much. In her mind, the woman was a witch. But Luna never said it aloud to her mother.

Edna shook off her thoughts, and looked at Luna. She knew her daughter was beautiful, with brown eyes, auburn hair, and a lovely face. Although she liked to wear jeans with T-shirts, she was still an attractive girl. Another three years and the boys would be after her for sure. Edna smiled to herself. She would have to be more aware of her daughter's movements. She decided to take Luna and go to the shopping center.

"Luna, go dress up. We're going shopping," she announced. Luna jumped off her chair and hugged her mother.

Edna and Luna walked to the shopping center. There, Edna bought groceries at her favorite shop. Jeb, the owner, always gave her discounts. He had always liked Edna. Jeb knew Edna was a good woman, and her work was always perfect. She was raising her daughter well. Luna was a delightful girl.

Once back in the house, Luna sat down with her school books while Edna began preparing dinner. As she cooked, her thoughts wandered. She remembered her husband. He wasn't a bad man, but he had some character traits that she now realized were the reason for his disappearance without warning. He had told her he was going to look for a better job and would be away for several days, but he had never returned. Had he married someone else? Edna sighed. It was likely she would never know.

The problem was Luna. She needed a father figure. Edna was trying her best to fill in that gap, but it wasn't easy. Luna had asked a few times where her father was, and Edna had tried her best to answer that question. Her father had gone away to work. After a couple of years, Luna stopped asking about her father. She had probably realized that her father had left them. When her friends at school asked her why her father never came to pick her up, she told them what her mother had told her—her father worked far away.

Edna dismissed the memories that threatened to flood her mind and concentrated on her cooking. She had never thought of remarrying. She would raise Luna by herself. And as far she could see, she was doing a good job of it.

She went back into the room where Luna was studying. Luna looked up at her mother and said, "Mamma, you're going to the mansion tomorrow?"

"Yes, dear. I will go and see what they say. It's a large house, and I'm a little worried about the amount of work they may want done."

"I will go with you, Mamma, don't worry," promised Luna.

Edna smiled. "Yes, of course, dear. But you have school to think of."

"But school finishes at one!" replied Luna.

Edna just nodded her head. "Why don't you have a piece of cake?" she suggested, diverting the topic. She would decide her course of action after meeting with the Samuelsons.

"I will, if you sit with me and have one too," said Luna, getting up to go to the kitchen. Edna laughed and a feeling of happiness swept over her. God bless her daughter! God bless her home!

As mother and daughter sat eating cake, a benevolent peace seemed to descend on the house.

After dinner, Luna sat down to read her story book. Edna picked up a magazine, an old one she had collected from one of the houses where she worked. She had acquired quite a collection of magazines. In them, she read about people who seemed to lead blessed lives, full of beautiful clothes, fast cars, and most of all, a lot of money. She often wondered what it might feel like to have that kind of money. She was sure Luna would grow up and work in a big company and earn a lot of money. Then, she would have a better life. That was the dream she was living. Weariness overtook her and she fell asleep.

The next day, Edna presented herself at the mansion. Mrs. Samuelson was courteous and kind. She said she had heard how good Edna was at her work, and Edna agreed to take the position. The pay was very good.

Luna was overjoyed at the news. She would accompany her mother to the mansion tomorrow.

The next day, as soon as Luna made it home from school, she changed and got ready to go with her mother to the mansion.

Edna was a little apprehensive. It was her first day. The house was large, set amidst sprawling grounds. As Edna and Luna arrived, they were met by a maid and invited inside. Luna gasped as she saw the large living room, with a stairway leading up to the second floor.

Edna and Luna set to work. Luna was busy cleaning the bannister of the stairway when she saw a boy about her age staring down at her. The boy had tousled hair and a smile on his lips.

Luna just stared up at him.

"What's your name?" asked the boy.

"Luna. What's yours?"

"Aiden. Want to play?"

Luna shook her head.

"Why not?" the boy asked, coming down and standing near Luna.

"I have work to do," she said, now aware of the boy's physical presence.

"I will wait. Once you finish, we can play." With that, he sat down on the stairs.

Thus began a friendship that carried on despite the fact that the two friends had dramatically different socio-economic backgrounds.

Two years passed, and one day Aiden, now 15, invited Luna, now 13, for a picnic on the golf course that lay behind the mansion. As they sat munching the sandwiches Aiden had brought, the talk veered around to what each of them wanted in life.

Luna wanted to graduate with high grades and work and earn good money. She wanted to give her mother a good life. Aiden sat in silence. Luna then told him about her father and how he had left them when she was only five years old.

"Don' t worry," Aiden promised. "I will always be there for you. Wherever you are!"

Luna was a little surprised at this. "You know, my mother doesn't like me meeting and playing with you. She says you're rich and I am poor."

Aiden considered this for a few seconds, then replied ruefully, "My parents don't like it either, but I don't care. You are my friend forever and ever."

"You're the only boy who wants to be my friend. At school, all the boys just ignore me. They say I'm tomboyish," said Luna with a sigh.

"So what? I think you're beautiful," Aiden confessed.

Luna felt a thrill pass through her body, such as she had never experienced. It was at this moment that Luna fell in love with Aiden. He would be there for her. He would protect her.

Aiddn reached out and took Luna's arm. "When we are a little more grown up, let's run away together."

Luna, too stunned to reply, just nodded her head. Then she thought of her mother. Leaving her behind was not something Luna wanted to do.

Within seconds, she made up her mind. She would take her mother with her and the three of them could live happily.

Life, Luna thought, was looking good.

The next day, Luna took with her a family heirloom, a small carved box, and gave it to Aiden. The heirloom was given to her by her mother. Aiden was surprised by this unexpected gift, but promised to guard it with his life.

Luna and Aiden made a pact. After completing university, they would elope.

Little did Luna know that fate had other plans for her.

Chapter 3

Standing in the pit, Luna held her breath. Was that a voice? She flattened herself against the wall of the pit and looked up in terror. It was entirely possible her mind was playing tricks on her. What were the chances someone else would be on this mountain during a storm? Was she going to be buried here?

Then, she heard a crunching sound.

"Hello, down there!" came a voice from the outside. Looking up, Luna saw a face. She couldn't see the details of the face, however, since the light was at the figure's back.

"Can you help me please?" she called desperately.

"Of course. Just wait, and I will lower a rope. Tie it firmly around your waist, then grab it with both hands. Can you do that?"

"Yes, I can do that," Luna replied. The Almighty had indeed heard her prayers.

The rope came down and Luna quickly tied it securely around her waist, holding onto it firmly. Her entire life depended on this rope.

Slowly, she was hauled up. As she reached the mouth of the pit, strong hands grasped both of her arms and pulled her out.

As she lay gasping on the ground, the man said, "Here, have some of this. Fix you up."

She looked up to see an extended hand holding a small bottle. She took it and drank a little, coughing as the whiskey hit her throat. Gradually, she began to feel life flowing into her hands and feet. She tried to stand up but her legs were not yet strong enough to support her. The terror she had just gone through seemed to have left her weak. It was her rescuer who pulled her to her feet.

"Take it easy, lady," he advised, steadying her.

Luna leaned on the man's arm; if she tried to move now, she would fall. The dread of the pit was still strong in her mind. She looked up at the man and said, "Thank you. You just saved my life!"

The man was bearded, and Luna could barely make out his nose and a part of his lips. A bushy mustache covered a part of his upper lip. He was wearing anti-glare goggles.

"Where do you want to go?" he asked.

"Gretchen. I have friends there," she replied. "But I seem to be lost. Do you know the way to Gretchen?"

The man nodded. "I do, but we can't get there in this weather. We need to find shelter quickly. We're too far away from the village," he explained. "Besides, you seem to have been heading in the opposite direction."

Something about the voice stirred a faint memory in Luna's mind, but it vanished quickly and she was unable to grasp it.

Her fierce independent spirit stirred. "Could you just point me in the right direction, please? I'll be able to reach the village on my own."

"Listen to me, lady, the storm will be extremely fierce within a few minutes. You will never reach Gretchen before it gets nasty. You'll be stranded. Come with me, I'll find shelter," said the man firmly.

Luna remained where she stood, undecided. She wasn't sure of the man's intentions. He had saved her life, but should she go with him?

The man seemed to have read her mind. "You think I will take advantage of your predicament? Well, suit yourself." He let go of her hand. "The village is that way," he added, pointing into the distance.

Luna could see nothing. Just a haze of white.

"Okay, then. Nice meeting you," said the man, turning to go.

"Wait, wait. I'll go with you. But how are you so sure that you can find shelter?"

"I know this area well. I will find shelter, trust me," he said, once again extending his right hand.

Together, they started moving. The storm was now raging with sufficient fury to make visibility almost zero, and Luna was just stumbling after the man. She didn't even know his name.

Luna's legs were starting to ache. Her breathing became a little heavy, and she began to gasp a little. Hearing her labored breathing, the man turned around and came to her side.

He stopped and looked at Luna. "Are you okay? The cabin is close. We can make it."

"Yes, yes, I'm fine," said Luna, relieved to hear that they would soon be out of the storm. "By the way, what's your name?"

"Benjamin," said the man, without turning.

"How do you know there's shelter here? And how far is it? I can't see a thing!" said Luna.

"Guess you'll just have to trust me on that," said the man easily.

After another 15 minutes of excruciating trudging through the snow, the man turned and pointed.

"Well, it looks like we made it," he said. Luna tried to see what he was talking about, and made out the vague outline of a structure in the swirling snow.

The journey from the pit had by now taken a toll on Luna's body. She was weary.

Thank God, she thought. At least now she could get out of this snow and wind. She needed to sit down and warm her body. As promised, Benjamin sure knew his way around.

When they got close, Luna saw that it was indeed a shack, or a cabin, whatever.

Benjamin pried open the lock and, with his shoulder, pushed open the door, signaling for Luna to get in. Inside, the rectangular cabin was quite roomy, though Luna could barely see in the dark. The light that came in through the single window to her left barely lit the room. But she saw at a glance that at the far end, there were what looked like cupboards and a table with something on it. What, she couldn't make out. She shivered. The inside was almost as cold as the outside. To her right was some kind of bunk. It was, she saw, covered in dust. Nobody had used this place in months, maybe even years.

The inside was a mess. Luna wrapped her arms around herself and looked around for a place to sit. She saw an old box covered with grime, and without much ado, she went and sat on it. She knew her pants would probably have to be discarded, but she didn't care. Relief coursed through her body. Benjamin, meanwhile, was trying to shut the cabin door to keep out the wind and the snow.

Luna sat and watched his desperate efforts. The snow pile outside seemed to be creating a problem. For a moment, she thought of lending a helping hand. She quickly realized she wasn't up to it. She just sat there and watched Benjamin struggling.

Luna's mind began to calm down, her breathing returned to near normal. She was uncertain as to what would happen now, or what she would do. Her thoughts turned to Frank.

Frank must be really worried by now. She pulled out her cell phone and checked for a signal, but there was none. Luna cursed herself for not going back with her boss when he'd suggested it. Now, she was stuck in a cabin with an unknown man, with what seemed to be a blizzard howling outside. Having noticed her attempts with the cell phone, Benjamin walked over and offered her the bottle of whiskey again.

"Here, have a tot. It will make you feel better," he offered.

Luna took the bottle and sipped a bit of the whiskey. She was feeling a lot better.

Benjamin had started messing around at the back of the cabin. There seemed to be a lot of stuff there covered by a tarpaulin. Luna watched as he yanked off the tarp and, using a flashlight, began examining the items.

"The generator may work," he said, and, bringing the tarpaulin, he spread it on the floor in front of Luna and sat down. "The cell phone won't get any service until the storm dies down, but there's a radio here, too. If it works, we may be able to use it to get in touch with others," he added hopefully.

Benjamin seemed quite calm as he took a drink from the bottle. Luna, by now, was feeling a little more confident—and she couldn't stop thinking about the people who would be looking for her.

"I have to inform my friends in Gretchen," she insisted. "They'll be worried sick."

"I understand, but what can you do?" replied Benjamin, standing up. "Let me work on the generator. By the way, what's your name?"

"Sarah," replied Luna, giving her daughter's name. She didn't want to disclose her real name yet. She didn't know this man, and she decided not to reveal any personal details. There were dangers to that. He might begin stalking her in the future. Who knew?

Luna's mind began to wander back in time to another cabin in another place—a holiday excursion with her husband, Marcus. Sarah hadn't yet come into their lives. They had sat and drank wine and laughed and joked all the time. She remembered Marcus's attempts at trying to get the high altitude stove to work. And their efforts at learning to ski. She had taken a tumble, and Marcus had laughed—and taken a tumble of his own at his next attempt. Luna smiled to herself. They were happy times. The cabin she remembered was larger than the one she was in now, and, of course, better furnished. But she was thankful for this one. It was a shelter.

"I think I can get this baby to start," Benjamin said, still fiddling with the generator.

Moments later, Luna heard a sputter and then a roar as the generator began to run.

Benjamin came and stood in front of her. "Now we'll be warm. You hungry?" he asked, pulling out biscuits from his backpack.

Luna was daydreaming and Benjamin's abrupt question brought her back with a start. "What did you say?" she asked.

"Do you want some biscuits?" said Benjamin, holding the packet in front of her.

Luna took it and extracted three biscuits before returning the packet to Benjamin. She was, she realized, quite hungry. As she munched on her biscuits, she began to study the man who was sitting on the floor, eating his snack without a worry in the world. The cabin was now quite warm, as the heater had begun to work.

There was something about him, something familiar. Without the goggles, the face she saw was strong. Not a man you trifled with, she thought. His eyes were a light blue, and the hands holding the biscuits were definitely capable, protective hands—the kind that had enormous strength, thought Luna.

"Since we're going to be here all night, we might as well get to know each other. What do you say?" Benjamin suggested.

"My name is Sarah, I already told you. What else is there to tell?" replied Luna.

"What do you do? Do you work?" asked Benjamin, looking at her.

"Yes, I work. For a finance company."

"Ah! Then you must be rich! I had that figured when I saw the clothes you're wearing. Expensive stuff, those," said Benjamin, a little mischievously.

Luna felt irritated. What was this man on about? She felt an even greater sense of annoyance when she saw the mocking look on his face.

"Annoyed, are we?" asked Benjamin. "Just trying to be friendly. That's not a crime, is it?"

"No, it isn't. You saved my life and that's a debt I owe you."

"And how do you propose to repay me? The debt, I mean."

Luna blushed furiously at the implication of the words. Benjamin's open-hearted laughter put an end to her doubts and she realized he was pulling her leg.

Pulling herself together, Luna said, "You said you would get the radio going. Where is the radio, anyway? I don't see it."

"It's at the back. We need to wait a bit. The weather outside is so bad that it won't work."

Benjamin stood up and, brushing the dirt of the tarpaulin as best he could, asked Luna to lie down and rest a bit while he worked on getting the radio up and running.

Without argument, Luna lay down and fell asleep almost immediately. And she began to dream.

Chapter 4

Sixteen years ago...

The blow fell on a Friday. Edna had just finished work at the mansion when Mrs. Samuelson came down and told her that her services were no longer required. As the woman handed her a month's extra wages, Edna just stood there, too stunned to utter a word. She felt her world crashing around her. She walked out of the mansion and back home in a daze. Luna wasn't home yet. She had finished high school and was trying to get into college.

Edna sat down to think. What could she do now? There were no more places nearby where she could find work. And with the wages she got from the two houses where she was currently employed, she wouldn't be able to cover her home expenses, let alone Luna's college tuition. Why had the Samuelsons fired her? She always did her work diligently. She got up and made herself some coffee. What was she going to tell Luna? That she couldn't go to college?

She suddenly remembered the owner of the shop where she usually bought groceries telling her that lots of new houses had been built to the north of town. And there was a demand for housekeepers, as the owners were mostly wealthy people. Finishing her coffee, Edna set out, locking the door behind her.

Jeb was in his shop and Edna told him about her situation. He was sympathetic; he liked Edna and knew she was an excellent housekeeper.

"The first thing is to get you a place to stay in the area," he said, picking up his phone.

After making a few calls, he put down the phone and smiled. "I've got you a nice two-bedroom place. Rent is cheap, and the landlord is a very nice older gent."

Edna stood undecided for a minute or two. A move would mean uprooting her home.

Jeb understood her reluctance. "Edna, there is nothing for you here. Go north and you will find more work than you can do. You will earn more. And your daughter can go to college. Isn't that what you want? Besides, I have friends there—they'll help you get work."

Edna nodded and thanked him, then left the shop and headed home. She was dreading having to tell Luna. As she neared her house, she saw lights. Her daughter was home. Edna braced herself. As soon as Edna walked in, Luna knew something was terribly wrong.

"What's the problem, Mamma?" she asked.

Edna sat down and recounted the events of the day. Luna remained silent for a bit.

"I know why they fired you," she finally said.

"You do?" Tell me."

"It's because of my friendship with Aiden," said Luna sadly.

Edna sat up straight. "I knew your friendship with that boy would lead to trouble."

"But Mamma, Aiden wants to be friends with me. He doesn't care what his parents think!"

"Luna, Luna—it's his parents who pay my wages, not Aiden."

"So, what are we going to do now?" asked Luna.

"We are going to move a little to the north. I've found a place for us to live in, and there's a lot of work in that area. It's just a few miles to the north from here."

"You mean, leave this house?"

"Yes. I need proper work and I need enough money to send you to college."

Luna was quiet. Moving away from here meant moving away from Aiden. She quietly left the room and went into the kitchen to prepare coffee for her mother.

The next day, Edna went to work and informed her current clients that she would not be able to continue. She collected her salary for the days she had already worked, and Mr. Richards, the owner of one of the houses she worked at, quietly gave her an additional sum of two hundred dollars. Edna was grateful for this extra income. Moving house was going to cost. After work, she went to meet Jeb. She told him that she had decided to move, and asked if she could go and see the place he had found. Jeb agreed, but said he would take her on Sunday, when the shop was closed.

***

As she sat in the car that Sunday, with Jeb driving, Edna looked around. The scenery around her was almost the same: the trees to the left and the river to the right. The house was small, almost similar to the one she was staying in at the moment but with a bit more space. The two rooms and the kitchen were larger. Edna liked the place and she agreed to move in at the beginning of the next month. Jeb introduced her to his friend, who said that work was not a problem—there was as much work as she wanted.

Edna and Luna began packing their meager belongings. Jeb would be taking them in his car to their new house. Their furniture would be delivered in a moving van, which Jeb had also organized.

The next Sunday, Edna and Luna got into Jeb's car. The moving van would follow the car. They took a last look at the house that held so many memories. As Jeb drove them to their new home, Edna was silent in the seat next to him, and he respected her silence. Luna sat despondently at the back.

As the car began passing the guard rails of the mansion, Luna saw Aiden standing on the golf course. She leaned out and yelled his name, but he didn't seem to hear her frantic voice. The car moved past the property and Luna slumped back onto the seat. She knew a very happy part of her life had just ended.

As Edna and Luna settled into their new home, Edna began working. She had jobs at three houses, and the pay was far better than what she had been earning before. She was beginning to think that the move was a good idea. Meanwhile, Luna had begun applying to colleges. She wanted to take up finance as her major. Within weeks, she was admitted to Baruch College.

After a nearly tearful farewell, she crossed into New York to start the next part of her life. Edna was cheerful and happy. This was what she wanted more than anything else. She thought of taking on an additional housekeeping job, but decided against it. If she fell ill, and lost her existing jobs, Luna would probably have to leave school. And Edna was determined not to let that happen. Her daughter would complete college and become someone, someone with a better life.

Luna took to college like a duck to water.She quickly made friends. Life was a little hectic, but slowly she settled in and started doing well. It was during her second semester that she met Marcus. Tall and handsome, he made excellent company. Over time, Luna and Marcus developed a friendship, and Luna felt attracted to Marcus, although the images of Aiden kept invading her thoughts.

Four years passed by, and Luna and Marcus were in a serious relationship, and both had landed jobs as soon as they passed out of college. Luna was hired as an executive at a financial firm, and Marcus was recruited by a tech company, in keeping with his expertise.

One day, while Luna and Marcus were having dinner to celebrate their new life, Marcus popped the question. Although a little surprised, Luna had accepted.

Edna, when she heard the news, was overjoyed. All her dreams were finally coming true. She had come to visit Luna on a few occasions before, but her work did not allow many holidays.

The day Luna and Marcus were married, Edna wept with happiness. After the wedding, Luna asked Edna to stop working—she wanted to look after her mother. But Edna refused. If she stopped working, she would have nothing to do, and that was a depressing thought. And if she remained idle, she would just grow old quicker. Luna was exasperated, but she gave in to her mother's decision.

After eleven months, Luna gave birth to a baby girl, whom she named Sarah. Then began the complicated process of juggling work with the raising of the baby. But Luna was tough, and although it was stressful, she managed it. Sarah slowly grew into a beautiful girl, and at age seven, she was already popular with everyone who met her.

Luna, however, began to feel that Marcus was staying out longer than usual. She began to disbelieve his excuse of work keeping him away, especially in the evenings. She realized that mentally, they were drifting apart. She started to feel a sense of claustrophobia, and decided she needed to get away for a few days. The problem was Sarah, her precious daughter—but she knew she could rely on her mother to help out. Marcus seemed unconcerned about their home. Buying groceries and the rest of the work was almost all her concern. Luna began to sense that Marcus's attention was directed at something or someone else. But she kept quiet. She had no proof.

***

"Hey, Sarah, wake up!"

Luna awoke with a jerk. She looked up to see Benjamin holding a mug of coffee.

"Where did you get coffee from?" she asked, accepting the mug gratefully.

"A gift from the Almighty!" said Benjamin, sitting down on the box, and Luna couldn't help smiling. "Okay, Sarah, now let me ask you something. How did you come to be in the mountains all alone? You don't seem to know the area at all."

"I wasn't alone. There was someone with me," replied Luna.

"Your husband. Or was it a boyfriend?"

'That's none of your business," she retorted angrily.

"Hey, don't be so touchy," said Benjamin with a grin on his face. "The point is, why did he leave you here?"

Seeing his grin, Luna felt her irritation increase. "He didn't leave me, I told him to go back. How was I to know that I would get stranded by a storm?"

"And fall down a hole," added Benjamin, teasingly.

"Thank you for reminding me!"

"No thanks required. So, are you married, have kids?" said Benjamin in a conversational tone.

Luna was annoyed at his question. "That's a bit personal. Gentlemen never ask personal questions of a lady."

Benjamin got up and started prowling around. "I'm single. Have my own business, but my uncle runs it. I live in a large house and do a lot of traveling. That's me in short."

Luna listened with interest. "So, you don't work for a living?" she asked.

"I do, but not all the time. I put in some hours every week. But it's my uncle who actually runs everything."

Luna was beginning to feel that somehow, Benjamin was familiar. Where had she met him before? She closed her eyes and tried to think.

Moments later, she opened her eyes to see that Benjamin was nowhere to be seen.

"Benjamin!" she called out, confused.

"Checking the toilet, to see if it works," he called from the other room. "The heater seems to have defrosted the water in the storage tank."

Luna walked to the rear of the cabin and saw an open door. Inside, Benjamin was busy with a brush, scrubbing the wash basin. The toilet looked clean enough. Luna realized that she needed to use it.

"Mind stepping out? I need to use the washroom," she said.

When she came out, Benjamin was busy fiddling with the radio. Luna wasn't very confident that it would work, but Benjamin seemed to know what he was doing. She walked over and sat on the box. The cabin was now quite warm, and she felt a sense of comfort.

"We need to get the radio going so I can inform my boss that I'm okay. Then I need to call home," said Luna.

"So the guy who was with you was your boss?" said Benjamin without turning around.

Luna realized that denial would be useless. "Yes, he's my boss."

After a few minutes of silence, Luna was convinced that the radio was dead. Still, she waited anxiously for Benjamin's diagnosis.

"I think I can get the radio fixed. Just hope it doesn't blow out," said Benjamin, still bent over the radio set.

After a few minutes, Luna heard the static crackle. She stood up and went over to where Benjamin was working on the radio.

"It seems to be working!" said Luna.

"Yes. Now to see whether we can get any info about the storm!"

The voice that came over the radio was slightly distorted, but the words were intelligible. According to the speaker, the storm would take another day or two to dissipate. All residents of Gretchen and the surrounding area were advised to stay indoors.

The announcement stunned Luna. Two more days in this cabin! A sense of panic gripped her. What was Marcus thinking? What was Frank thinking, for that matter? She desperately needed to contact them to let them know she was alive and well.

Benjamin, noticing her distress, got up and walked over to her. "Don't worry, everything will be fine," he said in a confident voice, which did nothing to pacify Luna. "Let me make some coffee. The cell phone might work once the cloud cover disperses a bit," he added.

"And when will this bloody cloud cover disperse? Any ideas?" she almost shouted.

"Tomorrow morning, hopefully."

Luna sat down and held her head in her hands. The throbbing in her head was getting worse.

Benjamin was busy with a saucepan. He was heating something.

"Drink this. And try to relax. There's nothing we can do. We just need to ride out the storm," said Benjamin, handing Luna the coffee. "I have canned food in my knapsack, and there is some stuff in the cupboard here, too."

"Meanwhile, let's talk. Sitting and moaning won't change anything," said Benjamin evenly.

"What should we talk about? And by the way, where did you get coffee from?" Luna murmured.

"Well, since you seem a little cagey about your personal life, let's talk about what interests us both. I like to travel, visit places, climb mountains, and make model ships and airplanes," said Benjamin. "And I carry coffee with me in my backpack."

"I work, I'm interested in cinema, and I like to travel, too," said Luna, carefully choosing her words. The unsteady light in the cabin was beginning to affect her. From the window, she could see that it was dark outside, and the only sound was from the howling wind.

Chapter 5

Luna began to look around the cabin.

Benjamin was watching her. "Don't worry, Sarah. You'll have privacy when you bed down for the night."

Luna blushed. "That's not what I was thinking!"

"Yes, you were," replied Benjamin, getting up and moving toward the door of the cabin.

That was when Luna saw the thick plastic slats pushed up against the wall. Benjamin pulled on them and they formed a curtain, separating the cabin into two parts.

From the other side of the plastic curtain, she heard Benjamin. "The inside is your room. I sleep here," he added, poking his head out.

"But what are we going to sleep on?" asked Luna.

"I have a bedroll you can use, and there is a bunk here that I will sleep on."

Luna pushed the curtain aside and saw a bunk attached to the wall, supported by wooden beams and bolted to the floor. It looked kind of dusty.

"It's dirty," she said, pointing to the bunk.

Benjamin smiled and pushed back the slats, creating one large space again.

"I'll clean it. No worries," he said matter-of-factly.

Luna began to relax. Benjamin seemed to be a very capable sort of guy, she felt a little embarrassed at her attitude toward him. She looked at her watch and saw that it was 10 p.m. She was a little hungry.

"Can we warm up some food?" she asked.

Benjamin seemed to be busy organizing the bunk, but he looked up when she spoke. "Sure, we can. Feeling hungry?"

Luna nodded.

"But first, we need a drink," he suggested. "What do you say?"

"Where are you going to get liquor from?" asked Luna with a laugh. She pointed at the empty pint bottle lying against the wall. "That one is finished."

"Always carry alcohol with me when I'm in cold places. Alcohol can save a man's life," he declared, opening a zipper in his backpack and extracting a bottle of whiskey.

Luna was amused. "What else have you got in there?"

"Patience, lady, patience. Everything in its own time," said Benjamin, unscrewing the cap. "Better wash your coffee mug. There are no glasses here."

Luna got up and took both coffee mugs to the bathroom and washed them. When she came back, Benjamin was standing with the bottle in his hand. Luna placed the mugs on the box; it was the only table they had.

As he poured the whiskey into the mugs, he said, "Feeling a little more at ease, are we?"

Luna laughed out loud. "Yes."

"That's great," replied Benjamin, handing one mug to Luna. "Not all men are beasts, you know." He laughed. "Here, sit down on the box."

As Luna sat and sipped her whiskey, Benjamin rummaged in his backpack, opening and closing zippers. What was he doing?

Benjamin pulled out a small packet. "Peanuts!" he cried exultantly.

Luna realized she was actually enjoying herself. She took some of the peanuts and started chewing. This man was an excellent companion; he seemed confident and calm. Not once had he shown any signs of stress or anger, and he was good with his hands. Luna knew that he would get the radio transmission to work—he had already managed to snag some broadcast that warned of the storm. And she desperately needed to send out messages by radio or cell phone, whichever worked earlier.

"The outward transmission still isn't working. Possibly because of the storm."

Luna sighed. No cell phone and now no radio.

It was time to make up for her suspicions and attitude toward her savior.

"So, Benjamin, what sort of business are you in?" she asked.

"We deal in building equipment. We have several warehouses and offices all over the U.S.," he replied.

"Wow! That means you really are a wealthy man," said Luna, trying to understand whether he was joking or being serious.

"Yep, I have lots of money. But I didn't make all of it. Some of it, I inherited."

"Lucky you!"

"If you say so," said Benjamin, in a bantering tone. He was studying her very closely.

Luna held out her now empty mug. "Can I have another?" she asked.

"Sure." Benjamin leaned over and poured her another shot of whiskey. "I'll go rustle up some dinner. You sit and enjoy the drink."

Luna offered to help, but Benjamin firmly declined her offer.

"I'm very good at this," he assured her. "Just sit."

Luna heard him opening the wall cupboard at the back of the cabin. After a minute, he walked back to his backpack and, unzipping a compartment, took out several tins.

She stared in amazement. What else was there in that magic backpack? Without a word, he carried the tins to the back of the cabin, and Luna saw the stove was alight.

He went into the bathroom and she heard the sound of something being washed. His measured movements and his ability to just get things done entranced Luna. She thought about her husband. If Marcus had found himself in this situation, he would be completely flummoxed. He could hardly make an omelette properly. His idea of food was of the packed and ready-to-cook type—shove it into the microwave and bingo! She wondered what type of garbage he was eating, now that she wasn't there. Sarah, thank god, was probably at her mother's by now. The nanny she had engaged for her daughter was likely enjoying an unexpected vacation.

Moments later, her thoughts were interrupted by Benjamin. He was holding a slightly bent fork and a spoon in his hands. "Take your pick," he announced with a flourish.

Luna picked the spoon, which appeared to be in better condition than the fork.

"The dish is baked beans with canned meat. Do you want to eat from the saucepan or the tin?" asked Benjamin.

"The saucepan, please," replied Luna. Well, this was going to be some experience.

Benjamin brought her the saucepan and settled down with the can from which he had decanted the beans. Luna looked at the saucepan and saw that the mish-mash looked good. It smelled good, too. She began to eat hungrily.

After she had finished, she got up and went to the bathroom to rinse the saucepan and the spoon. Benjamin was still digging into the can with the fork, and Luna watched him eat.

Once dinner was over, Benjamin brought out a folded package, removed the tarpaulin, and laid out what appeared to be bedroll.

"That's your bed for tonight." he said, picking up the sheet and walking toward the door end of the cabin. He drew the curtain, and Luna found herself alone.

"Good night!" she called out, and she made herself comfortable and lay down to sleep. But images of her past began to appear behind her eyelids.

She saw her mother and wondered what she was doing now. Edna was probably fast asleep; Sarah must be asleep, too. Then, her mind began to focus on Marcus. He was probably partying with friends. As sleep slowly took over, the last thought that crossed Luna's mind was that Benjamin would have made a better husband.

When she woke up with a start, she felt a little disoriented as her current predicament slowly came back to her. She sat for a while. Where was Benjamin?

He finally appeared from behind the partition and stood with his hands on his hips.

"Wakey, wakey, it's 10 in the morning! Here, have some coffee."

As they sat drinking coffee, Luna once again felt a sense of comfort and security—something she hadn't felt for a very long time. This man was someone who could be relied upon, for almost everything.

"Thinking of home?" asked Benjamin.

"Yes," lied Luna.

"Well, the storm seems to be blowing over. We should have a clear sky by late afternoon, if the weather guys are correct," said Benjamin, looking out of the window.

"I need to contact Gretchen, home, and my mother," said Luna, pulling out her cell phone.

"That won't work now, so don't bother switching it on. Conserve the battery. I'll tell you when you can get a signal. The cloud cover has to thin out first, and it's still pretty dense. Take a look through the window."

Luna stood up and, with her face to the glass pane, peeked out. The sky was still clouded, the wind still quite stormy. All she saw was a blanket of white. *There must be more than two feet of snow out there,* she thought.

When her nose began to feel numb, she turned from the window and stretched herself. She was feeling fit and, to her astonishment, quite happy. Benjamin, she found, was busy with the stove. The cabin was actually fairly comfortable. It was old, no question, but the structure was solid. Benjamin had pushed the slats back to the wall and the cabin was once again one big room.

She rubbed her palms together. "Can I help with breakfast?" she offered.

"Nope. It's almost done. Baked beans and coffee!" replied Benjamin.

It was once again the saucepan and the spoon for Luna, and the bent fork and the can for Benjamin. After they had finished eating, Benjamin stood up and said he would work on the radio. Luna realized that he would be almost next to the bathroom door.

"Could you just give me a few minutes? I need to use the washroom."

"Sure," said Benjamin, walking back to the box and sitting down.

In the bathroom, Luna lowered the toilet seat cover and gently sat on it. This man, Benjamin, was getting to her. She was attracted to him. *You have a family,* she reminded herself. But her growing sense of attachment to Benjamin kept coming back.

Luna decided to keep her distance from him, even though they were together in a single room. In any case, they would go their separate ways once this blasted storm blew over. She would be wise to watch her step.

She flushed the toilet and stepped out. Benjamin was still sitting on the box, humming a tune.

"Done?" he asked. Luna nodded.

Benjamin started working on the radio, and Luna heard odd crackling and whistling sounds. What a mess she was in! If only she had listened to Frank. He must be worried out of his mind by now. If only she could inform him that she was just fine. She wished she had something to do, anything to keep her mind occupied.

After a while, Benjamin came back and sat down on the bedroll. "Just have to wait for the cloud cover to thin out. The radio works, but I can't get a signal out," he said, sounding a little crestfallen. "We just have to wait for Mother Nature to calm down."

"You did your best," said Luna. "Let's just be patient."

Benjamin looked at her and smiled. "You seem to have come to terms with the awkward situation we're in. That's good."

Luna was starting to notice similarities between Benjamin and Aiden. Her thoughts went back to Aiden and their last meeting. Aiden had promised to look out for her, always. She smiled to herself. Well, Benjamin was doing exactly that.

As the morning wore on, Luna and Benjamin continued trying to get a measure of each other, and as a result their conversation was aimless and desultory in nature. Luna was guarded. Benjamin, on the other hand, maintained a chatty style. He told Luna of some of the trips he had taken, and the problems he had faced. But Luna was no closer to knowing him. The man was still an enigma. She decided to just act normal, but with a tad extra caution.

Chapter 6

At about one in the afternoon—although inside the cabin, time seemed to have stopped—Luna decided to take a bath. It suddenly struck her that she would have to wear the same clothes she had on, and that was a disgusting thought. And what would she use as a towel? She didn't have one.

Turning to Benjamin, who was still busy with the radio, she asked if he had anything she could use as a towel in that backpack of his.

Benjamin straightened and, without a word, went back to his backpack and started rummaging. He produced a small hand towel. "Use this."

Luna saw that the towel was barely two feet by two feet, but it was, she thought, better than nothing. Entering the bathroom, she saw there were no pegs of any sort to hang her clothes on. She would have to leave her clothes outside. The bathroom was small and she was afraid of getting her clothes wet—she had nothing else to wear. She opened the door and stepped out. Benjamin was still fiddling with the radio.

She poked him on the shoulder, and Benjamin looked up. "Not done already?"

"No. I want you to go to the bunk part, pull the curtain, and stay there until I call you. There's no place to hang clothes in the bathroom. I have to undress here."

Benjamin seemed to find Luna's statement hilarious. He laughed out aloud, raised his hands, and walked toward the front of the cabin. He pulled the slats and the partition was in place.

"And no peeking!" she shouted.

"Scout's honor!" agreed Benjamin.

Luna quickly undressed and entered the bathroom. She had a bath, using water sparingly. Once done, she used the towel to dry herself and stepped out.

Immediately, she saw Benjamin messing around with his backpack, apparently looking for something. Before she could jump back into the bathroom, Benjamin looked up and saw her.

Luna was angry, but as she was just about to say something, Benjamin stumbled back into the bunk area. She dressed quickly, then went and pushed the partition against the wall. Benjamin was lying down on the bunk with his eyes closed.

She stood there for a while, staring at the reclining figure. Then she began to laugh.

"Get up, you!" she said, pushing him.

Benjamin rolled over onto his side, his eyes still closed. "Can I open my peepers?" he asked.

"You know you can," said Luna, walking back and sitting on the box.

She saw Benjamin jump off the bunk and slowly walk toward her. He had a huge grin on his face.

"Scout's honor, was it?" she said.

"I promise you that I was looking for something. Seems to be lost though," said Benjamin, squatting on the bedroll.

"What were you looking for this time?"

"Never mind." Benjamin leaned back against the cabin wall.

"Hey! What did you lose?" asked Luna, and Benjamin just stared into the distance.

She felt sorry for him. This was the first time she'd seen him looking a little morose. His demeanor had changed noticeably.

She got up and laid her hand on his shoulder. "Is it valuable? Whatever it is that's lost?"

Benjamin didn't say a word. Luna sat down beside him.

"Where do you think you lost it? When you pulled me out or earlier?" she asked.

"Don't know. Anyway, nothing I can do now," he said, brightening up a little.

Luna and Benjamin sat together in silence, and Luna began to enjoy the closeness with this strange man. A sense of peace filled her mind and body. Benjamin stared straight ahead, and she wondered what he was thinking about.

Minutes passed in complete silence. Luna decided to make some coffee. Getting up, she walked toward the stove, next to the bathroom, and saw that Benjamin was already boiling water in the saucepan. The bottle of coffee grounds was half empty. She knew they needed to conserve the coffee. She made two mugs and came back, handing one to Benjamin, who took it without a word.

"How is it? As good as the coffee you made?" asked Luna.

"Too little coffee," he said matter-of-factly.

"We need to save some. No telling when we can get out of here. The bloody storm seems to be going on and on," said Luna.

"Yes, the storm doesn't look like it's over yet. I need to check the news. Let me run the radio."

Luna began to feel a sense of anxiety. Would the news be good? Or bad?

This time, she heard the transmission loud and clear. The storm system was still hovering over the area, and bad weather was expected to continue for the next two days. People were requested to remain indoors.

The blood drained from her face. Another two days stuck in this cabin? It would drive her crazy! Benjamin was sitting in front of the radio, staring at the ceiling as the transmission continued. He seemed to be taking the news calmly.

"What are we going to do?" exclaimed Luna.

"Nothing we can do," was the reply.

"Do we have enough food for two more days?" she asked.

"Yes. I have three more cans of meat, and there are four cans of baked beans here in the cupboard. That should see us through."

"Why didn't I listen to Frank!" she wailed.

"Pull yourself together, lady. We're going to see this through. Nothing is going to happen to either of us," said Benjamin with a sudden show of temper.

The outburst stopped Luna in her tracks—and she also heard the generator grind to a halt.

"Don't tell me the generator has gone kaput!" she said.

"No, it hasn't. I shut it down. It's old and needs rest. We need the thing at night, or else we'll freeze to death."

Luna felt disoriented again. What if the generator failed? She wondered how freezing to death would feel.

Would it be painful, or a painless oblivion? She closed her eyes.

A hand on her shoulder made her look up. Benjamin was standing next to her, a look of concern on his face.

"Sorry I yelled at you. You were going a little round the bend, and that's something we can't afford right now. I want you mentally alert," he said.

Luna just sat there, looking up at him. She felt the strength of his hand, gentle yet firm.

"Now, do you want to eat?" he asked, and Luna shook her head. She wasn't hungry yet.

Benjamin sat on his haunches in front of Luna.

"Listen to me very carefully. I want you to wear your coat, pull on your gloves, and put on your shoes. Then, you curl up and get some sleep if you can. Meanwhile, have a short sip of whiskey. Keep you warm.

"And stop worrying," he added, walking to his bunk. "These weather systems aren't very stable. The storm may blow over tomorrow."

Luna felt like telling him to lie down next to her and hold her tight, but she checked herself. Curling up into a fetal position, she tried to get some sleep, but found she was wide awake. She couldn't stop thinking of Benjamin.

He reminded her of Aiden. They had the same caring attitude, the same gentle demeanor. But she now knew there was a tough side to Benjamin. She had seen a small glimpse of his temper.

The cabin was beginning to cool a little. The generator was off, and so was the heater, but it was still comfortable.

She had to inform Frank and Marcus. Then her mother. She tried to think what she would tell them. She was staying with a stranger in a cabin, in the Swiss mountains? That would really put the fat in the fire! She knew her husband would not take that kindly. Every time she prepared to leave on a business trip, Marcus would look suspicious and ask her about where she was going, who was going with her, and so on. She decided not to tell Marcus. Not even her mother.

This was going to be her little secret.

Besides, Marcus never told her where he was most evenings. She knew he wasn't in the office. She had called the office reception phone and was told her husband had left. She had kept quiet, but she knew he wasn't working late. For the sake of Sarah, she kept things normal in the house, pretending to ignore Marcus's shenanigans. Well, this was one shenanigan that Marcus would never know about. A smile of satisfaction curled her lips. *Tit for tat,* she thought, *tit for tat.* She drifted off to sleep.

The sound of the generator woke Luna. It was dark outside, and she could still hear the sound of the wind. The storm somehow continued raging.

Benjamin was busy with the stove, and Luna guessed he was probably making coffee.

At least the generator was working. What a relief! They had a light in the cabin—not a very bright one, but a light is a light, thought Luna.

Sure enough, Benjamin returned with two steaming cups of coffee and handed one to Luna. On Benjamin's advice, they had dispensed with thank you. Luna just took the proffered mug and smelled the coffee. It invigorated her instantly.

Benjamin had placed the mug on the floor next to the box, and was once again ransacking his backpack. Luna just looked on. *What's with this guy and his backpack?*

He returned and sat on the box, holding a small packet in his hands. He began to unwrap the packet, smelled it, and then offered it to Luna.

"Biscuits!" Luna reached out and took one. It had gone soft, but it still tasted like heaven.

The stress of two people stuck in a room with nothing to do was beginning to get to both of them. Luna was trying to think of a neutral thread of conversation that would prevent her revealing personal details. But for the life of her, she couldn't think of any. The problem was resolved by Benjamin.

"Listen, we need to do something instead of just moping around in the cabin," he said.

What *could* they do, Luna wondered.

"How about word building? Know that game?" Benjamin asked, sitting down on the box.

Luna nodded.

"Fine. The rules are, you have to make words using the last letter of the word the last player said. And proper words, no vague stuff."

"I want to go first," said Luna, a little relieved that Benjamin had thought of something so innocuous.

"Rock."

"Kleptomania," replied Benjamin.

As the game progressed, boredom eventually began to set in again. And Luna was beginning to feel hungry. It was almost 9 p.m. How had time passed so fast?

Chapter 7

Benjamin prepared dinner with the same menu: beans and meat slices.

Luna sat on the bedroll and wondered when this incredible journey would end. She was sure Frank was panic-stricken by now, and probably blaming himself for leaving her. She tried to imagine his face.

The food arrived and Luna began to eat. Benjamin, too, seemed to be busy eating.

Luna watched him, wondering why such a handsome hunk of a man was roaming around single. He should have been snapped up by a woman by now. There weren't many like him. Good-looking, strong, and rich! An unbeatable combination.

Luna decided to have some fun.

"Why haven't you married?" she asked Benjamin, who by now had finished his meal and was washing the can and the saucepan.

Without turning around, he said, "I don't know. Haven't thought about it, I guess. Why?"

"Just wondering. You're good-looking and rich."

This time, Benjamin turned around and looked at Luna. "Ah! You find me good-looking, do you?"

Luna decided to take the offensive. "Yes, and you probably know that already."

"Is that a hint?" Benjamin asked, stroking his beard.

Luna knew she was in tricky territory. "No. Not a hint. Just curious."

Benjamin's response took her by surprise. "You see? That's why I'm single."

"What do you mean, that's why you're single?" she asked.

Benjamin didn't respond. He had finished washing up and had sat down in front of the radio set, which he continued to work on. Luna had no idea what he was doing.

She pulled out her cell phone, switched it on, and saw that the situation was the same. There was no hint of a signal. Sighing, she switched off the phone. Looking up, she saw Benjamin standing before her.

"I'm going to prepare some meat. Then we celebrate our predicament by drinking and singing and doing whatever else we can think of. To hell with tomorrow!"

Luna smiled. "Great! Let's do that. Is there enough booze?"

Benjamin went over to the cupboard and withdrew a bottle. He looked at it carefully. Luna watched him. The bottle was old.

She started laughing. "Good enough!"

Benjamin brought the two mugs and sat down next to Luna. He carefully poured the whiskey into the mugs and raised his own. "Cheers!"

Luna picked up her glass. "Cheers!"

Benjamin got up and returned with the saucepan and the usual spoon and fork. This time, Luna used the fork and started chewing on a piece of meat. It wasn't exactly gourmet food, but it tasted fine, albeit a bit smokey.

"Any good?" asked Benjamin.

"Mmmmm," murmured Luna.

"You eat, I'll go and check up on the weather," he said, and he walked over to the radio and sat down. Luna noticed that he had put on the headphones.

She continued to sip her whiskey and eat bits of the meat Benjamin had served up. But her mind was on the radio. She prayed there would be good news.

Benjamin, she saw, was listening intently, his head cocked to the right. To Luna, that signified bad news. Why wasn't he saying anything?

Minutes later, he put down the headphones and stood up.

"Is it good news? Or bad news?" she asked anxiously, bracing herself.

"Sort of half and half," said Benjamin.

"What do you mean?"

"The storm will start moving away by late afternoon tomorrow. But I'm afraid we can't move out before the day after."

Dear God, thought Luna, *another two nights here!* Benjamin, seeing her disturbed, came and sat down beside her.

"Hey! Am I that bad company?" he asked, putting his arm around her.

Luna stiffened. What was he doing?

She sat without saying a word. Benjamin removed his hand.

"It's not that. I'm worried about not being able to let people know. My boss must be going crazy with worry by now," she explained.

"Probably. But look at the situation realistically. We are stuck. We can't move out until this damn storm blows over. And even when it does, the snow is piled up God knows how high."

Benjamin's soothing tone of voice slowly reduced Luna's anxiety. She became aware of his presence, and his smell—a bit of sweat mingled with some odor she could not identify. She was alive with a sense of arousal. She got up and headed for the bathroom. Once inside, she closed the door and sat on the pot, trying to think. She wanted Benjamin.

Splashing water on her face, she leaned against the wash basin. She had to control her emotions. She had to.

Opening the door and stepping out of the bathroom, she saw Benjamin in a semi-reclined state on the bedroll. Seeing her, he straightened. "Not feeling sick, are you?" he asked.

Luna shook her head and sat down on the box, away from Benjamin. She didn't want to risk more sexual tension.

"Well then, drink your whiskey," suggested Benjamin, holding up the mug. "Let's be cheerful. Anxiety won't get us out of here."

Something inside Luna snapped. She decided to go with the flow. She took the mug and, in one shot, finished the contents. Seeing this, Benjamin rose up on his knees with an arm outstretched. "Whoa, lady. Easy does it!"

Luna held out her mug. "Pour me another one."

Benjamin hesitated before he poured her some more whiskey, holding back on the quantity. He was a little alarmed at Luna's sudden mood of defiance. He hoped she wasn't going to freak out. That would be awkward and difficult to cope with. He kept watching her looking for signs of mental symptoms. For the first time, he was a little apprehensive.

Benjamin decided to start a conversation. This silence was beginning to get to him.

"I was trapped in a hole once. Exactly like the one you fell into," he began, with a wave of his hands.

Luna took a sip of whiskey and looked at him. "Really? And how did you get out? Someone rescue you?" Her tone was flippant. The whiskey was beginning to take effect.

"I rescued myself," said Benjamin.

"Oh? And how did you do that?"

"At first, I didn't know what to do. It was a trekkers' trail, and not many people are around these trails. I waited and hollered for help for some time. Then, I realized that the chances of someone hearing me were zero."

Luna was following his words.

"After a while, I took out my multiplex knife and used the biggest blade to cut steps in the wall of the hole. It took me more than three hours to climb out of that pit. Of course, there was no storm."

Luna looked at him and said, "Not a very exciting story, is it?"

Benjamin laughed. "What I haven't told you is that the hole I fell into was not a hole but a crevice. These are deep cracks in the rock. Normally, falling into a deep crevice means death. But this one wasn't too deep. I was stuck between the walls, and had to pry my body loose before doing anything. I thought for a second I was a goner. But experience saved my life."

"So, if I had fallen into a crevice, I would be dead. Right?" asked Luna with a laugh.

"Absolutely," confirmed Benjamin.

"Are there crevices in this area?" she asked, back in control of herself.

"No. Not in this area," said Benjamin.

Luna fell silent and Benjamin decided not to disturb her. He was still a little worried.

As he stood up and stretched his arms, Luna said, "Let's play a game. That word building game isn't bad. At least it gives us something to do."

Benjamin stood for a while. "Okay. But let's use reward and penalty rules."

"What rules are those?" asked Luna.

"How about every time you fail to produce a word, you have to take off an article of your clothing?" suggested Benjamin.

"Oh no, you don't get me playing me a game with strip poker rules," said Luna. But she felt a stab of excitement.

"Why not?" said Benjamin. "It'll be like Vegas—what happens in the cabin stays in the cabin."

Luna sat silently.

"We're both adults. What is there to be coy about?" asked Benjamin, pouring whiskey into Luna's mug and pouring some for himself.

"That's not the point, is it?"said Luna.

"Well, what is the point?" asked Benjamin, lying down on the bedroll.

"I'm a woman!" she said, a little lamely.

"And I'm a man! So what?"

Luna tried to think of a rebuttal, but failed.

"Look, the most that can happen is that we may end up in bed," said Benjamin. "Either we play the game with an added spice, or we sit here and twiddle our thumbs."

"I don't want to go to bed with you!" she lied.

"Fine. Then once one of us is starkers, we stop the game," said Benjamin, sitting up. "I won't press you for sex! Scout's honor!"

"I don't believe you!" said Luna.

They continued to drink, and after a while, both were slightly buzzed. That was when Luna suddenly said, "Okay, let's play. Vegas rules."

The game began and as Luna discarded each item of clothing, she began to feel awkward, but she continued. Benjamin, too, lost several pieces of clothing, and was soon naked to the waist. Luna admired his rugged build. After she was down to her bra and panties, she realized through her alcoholic haze that Benjamin was much better at this game than she was. But she was beyond caring.

The game had gotten to a point where Luna was completely nude and Benjamin just had his briefs on. Luna was enjoying the compliments Benjamin was throwing at her. She was experiencing a mood she hadn't had before, one of complete abandonment. Even the overt sexual comments from Benjamin didn't worry her or even embarrass her. Benjamin had begun to sing—completely out of tune, as Luna would tell him later.

Without warning, he stood up and took off his jocks, and, grabbing Luna by the hand, said, "Let's shower together. We need to bathe."

Luna obediently got up. She knew what was coming, and even though she was quite drunk on the whiskey, she knew she wanted it.

In the bathroom, they poured water on each other, soaped each other, and Luna saw that Benjamin was in a state of complete arousal. She reached down and touched him. He pulled Luna toward him and held her in a tight embrace. Luna could feel his presence between her legs. Her hands moved to his groin and she held him. Benjamin's sudden exhalation of breath excited Luna even more.

They tumbled out of the bathroom and went to the bedroll. Luna and Benjamin made love with a passion that caught her unawares. Benjamin displayed a surprising knowledge of the erogenous zones; he seemed to know exactly where to touch and where to use his tongue. Benjamin bit Luna's nipples, holding each one in his teeth for several seconds.

Luna's excitement was at a fever pitch before wave after wave of orgasms hit her. She lost touch with the real world. There was only the sensation of pleasure.

Exhausted, Benjamin lay back. "That was the best!" he moaned.

Luna just lay there, savoring the contentment that flooded her body. Her breasts felt a bit sore, but that seemed to give her pleasure instead of pain. Then, the alcohol began to work its magic and both of them fell asleep, using their jackets and the bed sheet Benjamin had brought with him as cover.

Chapter 8

Luna woke with a start and, finding Benjamin's arm around her, quietly removed it and crawled out from under the sheet. She realized she was naked and quickly put on her clothes. As the first clouds of confusion passed, she tried to remember the events of the night before. She went to the bunk and sat on it. She needed to think.

When the full revelation of what she had done came upon her, she hid her face in her hands and started sobbing. She chastised herself for drinking too much whiskey. She should have known that disrobing before a man would ultimately lead to sex. She blamed herself for playing the game. It wasn't the liquor, but her own fault. As she tried to console herself, Benjamin came and stood before her, fully clothed.

As he began apologizing for what had happened, Luna got off the bed, pushed him away, and went and sat on the box. Benjamin was at a loss and stood for a while, trying to understand.

As Luna sat with her head down, Benjamin quietly walked over to the stove and made coffee. He brought it over and handed Luna a mug without saying a word. When Luna took it and began to sip, Benjamin went back to the stove and started heating the beans. He was hungry and Luna probably was, too.

Bringing the saucepan with the spoon, he placed it on the floor next to her and sat down on the bedroll to eat. Luna picked up the saucepan and began to eat, avoiding Benjamin's eyes.

"I am truly sorry about last night. It just happened," he said in a low voice.

Luna was silent. Benjamin ate quietly, and after he had finished, he went into the bathroom to wash up. He then sat in front of the radio and, putting on the headphones, started twiddling the knobs on the set.

Luna put the saucepan down on the floor.

Since Benjamin had the headphones on, she just sat and stared at the wall opposite. She could see through the window that it was still snowing outside. Her thoughts were in turmoil. She was unable to justify to herself her behavior the night before. Vegas rules, Benjamin had said. Well, nobody would probably ever know, but *she* knew what she had done. She would behave with extreme caution until she could get out of this cabin. At that moment, she turned her head and saw Benjamin looking at her. His demeanor was serious; the smile had disappeared.

"Why are you so upset? You aren't married and neither am I. So what happened last night wasn't such a great sin, was it?" he said.

"You wouldn't understand," Luna replied.

"Try me," said Benjamin, getting up and walking toward her.

"Please leave me alone!" she exclaimed, waving him away.

Benjamin walked away without a word. He was unable to figure out why she was so upset. Casual sex was commonplace these days. Each to his own, he thought and, shrugging his shoulders, sat back down at the radio and tried to get the transmission going. He also needed to be in touch with a few people—his uncle, for one. And the generator needed to be shut down. Fuel was running low, and there was no telling how long they would have to be holed up here. From what he had just heard on the radio, they would be here tomorrow and a part of the day after. That meant conserving food and fuel to last that long. And now he had a neurotic woman on his hands. Jeez!

Benjamin felt the sudden atmosphere of gloom that had enveloped the cabin. He asked himself if he was responsible? Possibly. But she had been game for sex, too! Why should he blame himself? He shook off the uncomfortable feeling and tried to see if he could get some other channel on the radio. Maybe listen to some music, to overcome the boredom. He felt Luna enter the bathroom but paid her no attention. *Let her come to her senses first,* he thought. He had done his best to apologize and she had just waved him away. It was consensual sex, for God's sake! Women!

Luna stood in the bathroom, feeling sick. She looked at herself in the small mirror above the wash basin. Aside from a little puffiness under her eyes, she was fine.

She had to stay another night with Benjamin, and after the intimacy of last night she was unsure of how to deal with him. Act nonchalantly or maintain a studied distance, interacting only when absolutely necessary? She would play it by ear, she decided, and stepped out of the bathroom. Benjamin was still busy with the radio, listening intently to something.

Luna just walked to the bedroll and sat down with her back against the cabin wall. She was determined not to do anything stupid. Was there any fresh news about this damned storm? She wanted to ask, but she realized that as he had his headphones on, he would probably not hear. She waited.

Benjamin took off his headphones and sat staring at the wall in front, feeling uneasy. The storm, he knew, would blow over by tomorrow night. They could probably leave the next day. But he had to spend two more days with a woman who was suspicious and nervous of his presence, and that was a bother. He heaved a sigh and got up.

"Anything new about when the storm is going to end?" asked Luna.

"We can leave the day after tomorrow. Midday, more or less, depending on the snow level outside," he replied, walking over to his bunk. He didn't even glance at her.

Well, thought Luna, *he has begun to keep his distance.* Still, the thought didn't give her any solace. She continued to sit, looking at the floor.

Benjamin, meanwhile, lay down on the bunk and started humming a tune. Luna decided to just ignore it.

But in the close confines of a sealed room, that proved to be difficult.

"Do you mind not humming?" she said.

Benjamin sat up. "Why? I'm not a great singer, I know that. But what else is there to do? If you don't like it, go to the radio and put on the headphones. That should do it!"

Luna felt her anger rising. This man was beginning to get on her nerves. She continued to sit, but the whistling sound of the wind irritated Luna. The situation had to be resolved. She walked over to the bunk where Benjamin was lying and extended her right hand.

"Friends again?" she asked, trying hard to smile.

Benjamin sat up, an amused look on his face. He shook Luna's hand and said, "We will always be friends."

Luna felt relieved. She leaned forward and kissed him lightly on the cheek, surprising Benjamin and catching him off-guard. He touched his cheek, and the smile turned into a gentle laugh.

"Gotten over it, have we?" he asked, getting down from the bunk. He took Luna by the arm and led her to the bedroll.

"Sit down. I'll make some more coffee," he said. Luna did as she was told.

As they sipped coffee, Benjamin chattered on about incidents in his life. Some happy, some not so happy. Luna listened with a growing feeling that this man was absolutely honest about himself. He didn't try to hide facts. He admitted his faults. What she didn't realize at the time was that she was slowly, but inexorably falling in love with this man. She watched in fascination as he went on talking, waving his arms about to emphasize his verbal content.

Suddenly, he stopped. "Now let's hear from you… what's your name again?"

Before Luna could stop herself, she said, "Luna."

"Luna? Really? I think you mentioned some other name before," he said.

Luna knew that she had committed a faux pas, and in a desperate attempt to make amends, she said, "Luna is my nickname. My proper name is Sarah."

But the damage had been done. Her secret was out.

Benjamin was now smiling hugely. "Lying to me, were you?"

Luna reacted with anger. "No, I was not."

"Okay, okay, calm down," said Benjamin.

The conversation, such as it was, came to a halt. Noticing that Benjamin was eyeing her with great attention, Luna began to feel a little uncomfortable. She cursed herself for not being careful.

"Well, tell me about yourself. You must also have tales to tell," said Benjamin, leaning back against the wall and folding his arms across his chest.

"I don't have an interesting life. I am what is called a working stiff."

"Everyone has some interesting experiences," murmured Benjamin, still staring at her.

Luna tried to think of something innocuous to say. She decided to relate the story of how they had to relocate because of her mother's job loss.

She started telling the story, careful to hide the location of their house, the one they had to vacate. Benjamin listened without interrupting even once.

"Your house was in a beautiful place, Hudson Valley, you said. Whereabouts in Hudson Valley?" Benjamin asked.

"Never mind which part. Why do you want to know?" replied Luna.

Benjamin, changing tack, said, "Your mother is a very brave lady. I would love to meet her. I admire people like your mother." After a pause, he added, "They can do the impossible."

Luna smiled to herself. Her mother was a tough lady, no question about that.

Benjamin abruptly got up and went to the window. Staring out for a few seconds, he turned to Luna. "The sky is clearing! Looks like we can go home soon!"

Luna got to her feet and stood by his side, looking out. She didn't see much difference. To her, it seemed like the sky was still a dismal gray.

"I can't see much of a change," she admitted, turning away from the window.

"You're not an expert, Luna. I am. There is definitely an improvement. The wind has shifted direction," replied Benjamin confidently.

Luna shrugged her shoulders and, undecided on her next course of action, went and sat down on the box.

Benjamin continued to stare out of the window. Then he turned and went to the generator. "Time to shut this down for a few hours."

Luna heard the generator slowly wind down. Suddenly, the silence became even louder. Luna could hear herself breathe. In the city, silence was a rare commodity, she thought.

Benjamin came and sat down on the bedroll.

"What do we do now?" he asked, scratching his head.

"Why don't you heat up some beans, and meat? I am a little hungry," said Luna.

"Sure. Why not," replied Benjamin, getting up. "At least it's something to do."

Luna looked at her watch and saw that it was three in the afternoon. Time was passing, she thought. Another 30-odd hours to go before she could go home. The events of the past 48 hours had taught her many things.

Benjamin came and handed over the saucepan and spoon. "Be careful, it's hot!" he said, sitting down on the bedroll to eat.

Chapter 9

As the evening wore on, Benjamin fell asleep on the bedroll, and Luna decided not to wake him. She went to the bunk and lay down. The temperature of the cabin was beginning to drop; the heater had gone off along with the generator.

Luna began to think of her daughter Sarah. What was the little darling doing now? Was she still at her grandmother's? And for that matter, what was Marcus doing? Having gala nights out? Possibly. She tried to get some sleep, but it eluded her. Her nerves were still highly strung and she could barely lie still. It was getting dark outside. What little light was coming in through the window was fading, and the cabin, too, was getting darker. She thought of waking Benjamin and asking him to crank up the generator. The growing shadows were beginning to lower her spirits even more.

She got up and poked Benjamin in the ribs. "Wake up, it's getting dark. Start the generator. We need light."

Benjamin opened his eyes and asked, "What time is it?"

"A few minutes past six," said Luna, looking at her watch.

Benjamin sat up and rubbed his eyes. He glanced around in the fading light.

Luna stood at the window, looking at the gathering gloom. *Will this never end?*

She heard the roar as the generator started and turned to see Benjamin making arrangements to prepare coffee. He had the stove alight and the saucepan on it.

As the light came on, Luna felt better. The heater had come on, too, and the cabin was beginning to warm up.

It was Benjamin who got the conversation going again. "So, what do we do now?" he asked.

"Drink coffee and talk," replied Luna.

"What about? I have emptied my stock of stories. You got any more?" said Benjamin.

"Not that I can think of," said Luna.

"There we are, then," replied Benjamin, coming over with the coffee.

"Let's talk about your fall into that crevice. How did you fall in?" asked Luna.

"Sometimes, crevices are covered by snow, and that makes them invisible. The crevice I fell into, well, it was totally hidden."

"It must have been a terrifying experience!"

"It certainly was. I thought it was the end of the line for me," replied Benjamin.

He leaned over and grabbed his backpack. Luna almost laughed out loud. The magic backpack again! What was he going to pull out this time?

Carefully putting his hand into one of the pockets, Benjamin withdrew what looked like a large phone. Putting that to one side, he pushed his hand inside once more and this time pulled out a packet.

"Ah! I thought so. I remember having at least three packets of biscuits."

Luna stared at the man in wonder. But the phone had caught her attention. "What is that? A cell phone?" she asked, pointing at the device.

"Yes, it is," said Benjamin, offering her the biscuits.

"That's the largest cell phone I have ever seen!" said Luna.

"Yes, it is rather large. But it's very powerful and can catch even a weak signal, which a normal cell phone, such as the one you carry, cannot," replied Benjamin, picking up the phone. "It's also heavy and solidly built. It doubles as a club in times of danger," he said, laughing.

He placed the cell phone on his backpack. "Better keep it outside. It might catch a signal later tonight."

This man was full of surprises, thought Luna. Interesting.

"I hope it does. We can both inform anxious relatives," she said.

"There's only one person I have to call, and that's my uncle," he said, looking away.

"Don't tell me you have no other relatives or loved ones you need to call!" exclaimed Luna, a little taken aback at this statement. Benjamin shook his head.

Luna felt a little sad. Not to have anyone close to turn to was a dreadful thought. What sort of life was he leading, she speculated. Was he one of those 'loners'? The type who trotted through life without building any permanent relationships?

Night had fallen, and outside, it was pitch black. Inside the cabin, Luna was comfortable, and importantly, safe. She felt a sense of gratitude toward Benjamin. He was responsible for saving her and giving her shelter.

Wanting to say something, she began to talk about her boss, Frank.

Benjamin listened, but he didn't seem particularly interested. His only comment was that her boss had left her by herself and gone back. Luna did not know how to react to that, and she fell silent. The conversation languished. For the first time, Benjamin appeared restless.

After a few minutes, Benjamin got to his feet and walked toward the back of the cabin. "Let me listen to the latest about the weather. If my intuition is right, the storm will move away by tomorrow morning," he said.

"I pray to God that it does!"

Luna moved about the cabin, trying to get the circulation back into her limbs. Prowling around, she began to think about what she would do first. Call Mamma? Or call Marcus? She would call her mother first. Sarah was probably with her. No, the first call would be to Frank—he must be informed that she was alive and well. That was priority number one. She just hoped the cell signal would return tomorrow morning.

She walked over to where Benjamin was sitting with headphones on. She bent down and asked loudly, "Any news?"

Benjamin raised his right hand, and nodded. Luna waited expectantly. When Benjamin continued with his headphones, she walked back to the center of the cabin and stood there, looking at Benjamin's broad back. He was a powerful man, she thought. Tomorrow, she would have to bid him adieu, and they would in all probability never meet again.

She felt a twinge of sadness. This man had saved her life. She began to relive the intimacy that she had shared with him. She couldn't deny how wonderful it had been. But her inhibitions prevented her from accepting it for what it was—a pleasurable experience. She promised herself that if he offered a drink, she would moderate her consumption. She didn't want a repeat performance.

Luna, tired of standing, went and sat down on the box. What was the man listening to, anyway?

Minutes later, Benjamin finally put down the headphones and came over to sit on the bedroll. The news he told Luna was good: tomorrow, they could leave. She was elated.

Benjamin pulled out the whiskey and poured himself a shot in the coffee mug, and looked up at Luna quizzically.

She lifted her mug and held it out. She wasn't going to behave like a prude. After he'd poured the whiskey, she realized she hadn't washed the coffee dregs from the cup.

They sat and sipped. Benjamin broke the silence.

"Tomorrow, God permitting, we leave. I'll have to check the snow level to see if walking is possible, but I think by midafternoon the snow will melt enough to allow us to move out."

Luna listened in silence.

"First, we go to Gretchen. I'll drop you off and then decide what to do," he said.

"Where do you plan to go from there?" asked Luna.

"Haven't decided yet," he said, pouring himself another drink.

Luna, to her stupefaction, suddenly realized she didn't want him to leave her. She wanted to be with him. She bit her lip in annoyance. What was happening to her? She held out her glass to distract her mind.

Benjamin poured the drink without looking at her. She was grateful for that. He would probably have guessed what was going through her mind.

Holding up his mug, Benjamin said, "Cheers! Here's to us!"

Luna joined in and smiled.

"Today, we have a grand dinner! A large helping for each of us. We don't need to be miserly anymore," he said, gulping down the whiskey and promptly pouring himself another one.

Looking at him, it occurred to Luna that she was definitely in love with this man. She began to dread their parting of ways.

Chapter 10

Benjamin served up dinner and Luna noticed that the portion was quite large. She wondered if she could eat all of it. Benjamin was using two cans this time—one wasn't big enough for the food he had served himself. Luna watched in fascination as he shovelled it into his mouth using the bent fork.

Once they had finished dinner, Benjamin picked up his cell phone and switched it on. He stared at it for a while.

"There's still no signal on this. I'll put it in silent mode and leave it out." He picked up his backpack and put it beside the bedroll, near the window. He placed his phone on the backpack.

Then, he wished Luna good night, pulled the slats into place to create the partition, and disappeared from Luna's sight.

Luna decided to try to get some sleep. Tomorrow would be strenuous enough; walking in knee-deep snow was not easy. But sleep eluded her until she was fed up of lying down. She got up and sat with her back to the wall. She would sit until sleep came. Looking at her watch, she saw that it was way past midnight already. *Better try for sleep,* she told herself and was about to lie down when she saw Benjamin's phone ringing.

She picked it up and saw "Ex Wife" as the caller. She quickly disconnected the phone without thinking and put it down. So Benjamin had been married. Why had he lied to her? She quickly pulled out her cell phone and switched it on, and to her dismay saw that there was no signal. Her mind raced. Should she use his phone and call Frank? *Better not,* she thought. Benjamin would see the number. And anyway, the signal on his giant phone was going on and off. She lay back down to sleep.

Luna heard footsteps, furtive ones. She kept her eyes partially closed and watched as Benjamin tiptoed to the bathroom. Should she confront him? She decided to wait until the next morning. An argument at this time of night would disturb whatever sleep she was going to get.

Luna woke to the now familiar shout of "Coffee!" She sat up and found that Benjamin was in a good mood, a bright smile on his face. After washing her face, she walked over and accepted the coffee. She noticed Benjamin's cell phone wasn't where it had been last night. Luna sat on the box while he remained standing, looking out the window. The light outside had grown stronger,and the sky looked a little brighter; there were specks of blue at the edges. The storm was passing.

"Why didn't you tell me you were married?" she asked with a spark of anger.

Benjamin turned abruptly and, looking at Luna, said," Who told you that?"

"Check your phone. Your ex-wife called last night."

Benjamin quickly retrieved his phone from the bunk and looked at the recent calls on the screen. His shoulders sagged. "Oh, bloody hell," he muttered.

Then, sitting on the bedroll, he looked at Luna. "We are separated and divorce proceedings are underway. It's been two years since I last saw her. The marriage, I can see now with hindsight, was a serious mistake."

"It's the woman's fault, is it?" said Luna.

Without hesitation, he replied, "No. It's my fault. She's not the type of woman I should have married."

"And what type should you have married?" asked Luna, a little facetiously.

"Your type."

The answer threw her completely off balance and she began groping for words. "Well, I hope you find someone," she said in a low voice.

Benjamin just shook his head and slowly stood up. "Let me check the news broadcasts."

As he sat with the headphones on, Luna began to wonder what sort of woman he had married. She couldn't for the life of her figure it out. This man was handsome and gentle. Maybe, she thought, he had another side to him. A bad side, a side she hadn't seen. But she brushed away the thought. She had now been with him for two days.

She decided not to pursue the matter further.

After a few minutes, Benjamin put down his headphones and walked over. He looked out the window, his hands in his pockets. Luna watched in silence.

"The divorce hasn't been finalized, but we have the basics agreed upon. Should be finalized soon," he said, still looking outside.

"Hope it works out amicably," said Luna.

"It's amicable, alright. She got what she wanted."

Luna, desperate to change the topic, asked, "What's the news? Can we leave today?

Still staring out of the window, Benjamin seemed lost in thought.

"We leave tomorrow morning. The snow needs to melt a little. We won't be able to walk through it today."

Luna let out a sigh. Another night here. She felt a sense of exasperation. Were the Gods putting her through some sort of test?

"Why can't we leave today? Walk slowly, maybe?" she suggested hopefully.

"No, we can't leave today. Too risky." Turning toward Luna, he said, "Want to fall down another hole?"

"No, of course not," she murmured.

"Then we leave tomorrow," said Benjamin in a tone of finality.

He rolled up his jacket and looked at his watch. Luna saw that it was a chronometer.

"It's about 10 now. Let's have a good breakfast. I will need to shut the generator down as usual," he said.

As the smell of beans and meat came wafting over, Luna hoped the cell phones would work soon. The light outside was improving rapidly, traces of sunlight beginning to appear. Benjamin had been right.

As they ate in silence, Benjamin was a little jittery.

"What's eating you?" asked Luna.

He seemed to be considering the question. "I think I'll try and find the thing I lost. I'm sure it's just outside the door. I must have dropped it when I pushed open the door," he said, nodding toward the front of the cabin.

"Oh, for God's sake! What have you lost?" Luna almost shouted.

Benjamin, taken aback by her outburst, looked at her curiously.

"It's a Swiss Army multiplex knife. I've had it for years. I'm somewhat attached to it," he said.

Luna couldn't believe her ears. "You're going to go out and dig through three feet of snow for a knife?"

Benjamin nodded.

"And what are you going to use to dig? Your bare hands?"

Benjamin laughed. "Don't know much about places like this, do you? There are always shovels for just such situations. There are two of them here."

He stood up and walked to the back of the cabin, and came back with a shovel. He unstrapped his watch and laid it on his backpack, next to his phone.

"As soon as I step out, close and bolt the door. I may need some time. Open the door when I knock. Okay?"

Luna just nodded. This man was really crazy. But she didn't say anything.

She walked with Benjamin to the front door and waited. Benjamin forced open the door enough to wriggle through. He pushed the door shut, and Luna bolted it. It was bloody cold outside.

As she walked into the middle of the cabin, her eyes fell on Benjamin's backpack. She decided to have a look inside, to see what else was there. She sat down next to it, removed the phone and the watch, and laid them beside her. Then she carefully and silently opened one of the main zippers. Inside, she saw clothes—not folded, just shoved in. She put her hands in and moved the clothes aside to see what else was there.

At first, she didn't see anything. Then, she noticed a small pocket with a zip, and it had a bulge. There was something inside it. She hesitated for a moment before she opened the zip, and with her fingers, she withdrew an object, a box. As soon as she saw it, she almost swooned. It was the box she had given Aiden! She sat back and the room began to spin around her.

Recovering her senses, she examined the box carefully. It was, beyond any shadow of doubt, the box he had gifted Aiden. How on earth did Benjamin get hold of it? It was then that the truth struck her. Benjamin was Aiden, there was no other explanation! She sat there in a daze, trying to comprehend. She remembered that she always felt that there was something familiar about Benjamin.

Another thought crowded her mind. Did he know that she was Luna, his boyhood sweetheart? Luna felt faint. She slipped the box into her jacket, zipped the backpack pocket, and pushed the clothes down. She carefully replaced the phone and the watch. Then she went and sat on the box, trying to steady herself.

As she sat, she could hear Benjamin digging away. She found to her astonishment that there were tears in her eyes. She quickly wiped them. This was no time for sentimentality. Her past had come back to haunt her.

Luna heard the knock and opened the door. Benjamin came in.

"Found it!" he said, holding up an object. Luna walked back and sat on the box. Benjamin followed her.

"Aren't you going to congratulate me for finding it?" he asked, sitting down and drawing his backpack close.

"Who are you? You are not Benjamin, that much I know," said Luna.

Benjamin was unzipping his backpack, but froze when he heard Luna. "What do you mean, who am I?" he said.

Luna leaned forward and said, "Your name is Aiden, correct?"

Benjamin scratched his head and remained silent.

"Are you Aiden?" Luna repeated, this time a little more loudly.

"Yes, I am. How did you find out?"

Luna brought out the little box and held it up. "I found this in your backpack. It's the box I gifted Aiden many years ago," she said.

Benjamin slowly came and stood before her. Luna stared at him, trying to find some features of recognition.

Walking away a bit, he said, "I knew you were Luna the day I pulled you out of the hole."

"Then why didn't you say so?"

"I wanted to see if you would recognize me. When you didn't, I let it ride. No point in dragging up old memories. And besides, you have a ring on your finger. That means you're married."

Luna looked at her hand and saw the engagement ring Marcus had given her.

Luna smiled. She looked at Benjamin, and this time saw Aiden. She wondered why she hadn't recognized him earlier.

"Does this change things between us?" asked Aiden.

"How can it? I'm married and have a daughter, Sarah, and you are in the process of a divorce," she said.

Aiden pushed Luna aside just a bit and sat down on the box. Luna moved to give him space. It was a tight fit.

"Are you happy in your marriage, Luna? Really and truly happy?" he asked.

"Why do you ask?" she replied.

"Well, look at it like this. You came here on a holiday with some guy from your office. Why didn't you come with your husband?"

"He's not some guy. He's my boss, and he is a gentleman," retorted Luna, now annoyed at Aiden's attitude. "And for your information, I just wanted some time away from the family, from my husband. That's all."

Aiden stayed quiet and, getting up, went across to the stove. He lit it and put on the saucepan. "You know, Luna, you're a bad liar. You always were."

This time, Luna stood up in anger and shouted, "I am not a liar!"

Aiden turned and looked at Luna. "Put your hand on your heart and tell me that you love your husband!"

Luna hesitated. She knew Aiden had put his finger on the exact spot she was trying to keep secret. For the last two-odd years, Luna had been slowly falling out of love with Marcus. It was as if he had changed drastically. He was no longer the loving and funny person she had married, and she suspected he was having an affair. In fact, she was sure. She just didn't know who the woman was.

Aiden came, sat beside her, and handed her the coffee.

Chapter 11

"Luna, I'm still in love with you. I never thought we would meet again. And now that God has brought us together, I have a proposition."

Luna sat rigid. She knew what was coming and a part of her wanted to hear it.

"Let's just go away and get married!" Aiden said impulsively.

"How can you say that? I'm married and have a daughter."

"Initiate divorce proceedings. I have a very good lawyer. It won't cost you a cent!" he said, sounding eager.

Luna looked sideways and saw the excitement on his face. He meant it.

"I don't want to break up my home," she said without much conviction.

Aiden got up and went to the bedroll and sat sipping his coffee. Luna looked away, trying to come to terms with what she had just heard. She knew she too was still in love with Aiden. And here he was in person, sitting in front of her.

Luna felt like running away; her emotions were in a state of turmoil. She wanted to sit with Aidan, have him put his arms around her. But she was trapped in a loveless marriage. A sob escaped her and Aiden was immediately by her side, his arm around her. Luna rested her head on his shoulder.

It was slowly getting dark outside when Aiden got up and restarted the generator.

As the lights came on, Luna got up and stood at the window. She was having a hard time trying to understand her feelings. Memories of her encounters with Aiden began flooding her mind.

Turning her head, she saw that Aiden was busy with the radio. She watched him with affection. The Aiden of her childhood had grown into a man—and what a man!

She walked over to him and put a hand on his shoulder. Aiden covered her hand with his own. Luna let his hand be and just stood there, savoring the sensual experience coursing through her body.

Over dinner, they talked about old times. Of their meetings, sometimes in secret. Luna relived the moments and found that the magic still remained. She was happier than ever before. Aiden, too, seemed to be enjoying himself.

When bedtime arrived, Aiden quietly withdrew to his side, putting the slats in place. Luna almost asked him to stay with her, but something held her back. Tomorrow, she and Aiden would part ways. She knew it would be painful for her. And Aiden? What would it be like for him?

Luna woke to find the cabin awash with sunlight. Outside, the sun was shining and the sky was blue. The storm had finally gone away. Luna got up and felt braced. The bright sunshine lifted her spirits immediately.

Aiden came over and gave her coffee. She looked at him and said, "Can we go outside for a bit? I am tired of this cabin."

He nodded, and together, they went outside. Luna felt a sense of freedom. She picked up some snow, made it into a ball, and threw it at Aiden. She got one in return. The snowball fight continued for a few minutes until Aiden put a stop to it.

"We need to pack and move," he said.

They packed up and Aiden closed the cabin door and locked it. Then hand in hand, they started toward Gretchen. Aiden seemed to know the way, and within the hour, Luna caught sight of the village. The first thought that came to her was about Frank. Was he still there? She was sure he was. He wouldn't leave her behind. Besides, how could he? The storm had affected everyone in the area.

Reaching the village, Luna saw that it was a busy day. Shops had opened up and people were going about their work. Luna headed for the hotel, with Aiden in tow.

The hotel receptionist was startled to see her and quickly ran upstairs to call Frank. Luna and Aiden stood there waiting.

Frank came down in a rush. "Jesus, Luna! You're okay?" were his first words. He came over to embrace Luna. Then, noticing Aiden, he said, "And who is our friend?"

Luna took Aiden's hand and said, "Frank, meet the man who saved my life!"

Frank shook Aiden's hand and led them to the lounge. Luna told Frank about what happened, and he listened, goggle-eyed.

"Lucky you met Mr. Aiden, then."

"God-sent, I would say," said Luna, winking at Aiden.

"Let's all have a bite to eat. After all, you guys have been eating beans for what, two or three straight days?" said Frank. "Let's go and sit in the restaurant. We can talk there."

They all moved to the restaurant and Luna ordered food. She noticed that Aiden hadn't said a word.

"Anything bothering you?" she asked.

Aiden turned to Frank and said, "Any way of getting to the airport?"

"Sure. You can come with us, we will be going there tomorrow," offered Frank.

Aiden thanked Frank, and went to the reception desk to see if they had a room for him.

***

The next morning, Luna and Frank were ready to leave, waiting for Aiden to come down and join them. When he appeared, they all got into the car and set off for the airport.

At the airport, Aiden asked Luna to step aside. He wanted a word with her in private. Luna signaled for Frank to move to the lounge, and she came and stood next to Aiden.

"I want you to think about my offer of marriage. Think about it seriously. I will be waiting for you. Remember that," he said, pulling out a scrap of paper from his pocket and handing it over to Luna.

"That paper has my mobile number, my house phone number, and my address."

Luna looked up at his face. "Bye for now, Aiden. Maybe we'll meet again."

She turned and walked away to join Frank. After a while, when she turned back, Aiden had vanished.

She needed to call Marcus. She had tried twice already, and on both occasions the call had gone to voicemail. Marcus hadn't answered. Luna was a little worried. Her mother had told her that Sarah was with her, and she had spoken to her daughter. She decided not to try Marcus again—she would just take a taxi from the airport and go home. Frank wanted to drop her off, but she refused. She didn't want company on the way home. She had a feeling that something was going to happen, something unpleasant.

On the flight, she found that Aiden occupied most of her thoughts. She wished she had kept in touch with him. She sighed, thinking that destiny must have had a hand in this. There was nothing she or Aiden could do. Frank, sitting next to her, noticed her somber mood but said nothing.

After the plane landed, Luna and Frank picked up their luggage and headed for the exit. Luna was able to get a taxi before Frank. She bade him goodbye and gave the driver the address, then leaned back and closed her eyes.

The taxi came to a halt and the driver, noticing Luna's closed eyes, said, "We're here."

Luna opened her eyes and saw that she was indeed home. She paid the fare and the driver put her bags on the pavement. Luna stood there for a moment as the cab drove off.

Then she picked up her bags and entered the building, heading for the elevator. At the sixth floor, the elevator came to a halt. Luna stepped out. Her apartment was the one in front of the elevator. She put her bags down and opened her purse. Extracting the key, she opened the door. The moment she stepped in, she heard the sounds of laughter. Both male and female.

Luna quietly laid the bags on the ground, making no sound at all. She recognized the male voice as that of Marcus, her husband. The female voice was unknown to her.

She tiptoed to the bedroom door and slowly opened it. Inside, she saw Marcus in the arms of a woman with turquoise hair. Both were naked. Marcus saw her first and covered himself with the bedsheet. The woman did the same, staring at Luna.

"Where have you been?" said Marcus.

"Get her out of here. Then we need to talk," said Luna, turning and leaving the bedroom.

She could see the bedroom door from where she sat in the living room. Moments later, Marcus appeared. He seemed a little undecided as to what he should do. Luna waited patiently, without uttering a word. She noted that the woman was still in their bedroom.

Marcus came over and sat down on a sofa opposite Luna. He didn't look at her.

"So, this is your game, is it? Bringing tarts into our bedroom?" said Luna with anger in her voice.

"She's not a tart. She's a decent woman." said Marcus, still looking away.

"She looks like a tart to me," countered Luna, now thoroughly enraged.

Marcus was silent.

Luna, pointing to the bedroom, shouted at Marcus, "Why is she still in there? I told you to get rid of her!"

Marcus now looked at Luna. "I love her and I want to be with her."

Luna was so taken aback by this bold statement that for a few seconds, she was speechless.

"Fine. Pack your things and leave the apartment. And take your tart with you. This place is in my name, and I decide who stays here and who doesn't," said Luna.

Marcus sat up straight. He wasn't ready for this salvo. "Okay. I'll leave in the morning. It's late," he said.

"No. Leave now. Now," insisted Luna.

Marcus got up and, in a burst of bravado, said, "I'll fight you for custody of Sarah."

He disappeared into the bedroom. Luna just sat there. Her world was falling apart.

After 30 minutes had passed, Marcus came out of the bedroom carrying a suitcase. Behind him was the woman.

"I'll come later to take the rest of my stuff," he said, heading toward the door.

"Leave the keys. When you need something, call me and make time. I don't want you coming here whenever you like. You don't live here anymore," said Luna.

Marcus threw the keys onto the floor and left. Luna just sat there. But it was too much to bear. Her emotions overcame her and she started crying.

When Luna quieted down, she wiped her eyes and went to the bathroom. She splashed water on her face and looked at herself in the mirror. She looked terrible.

She went to the liquor cabinet and found most of the liquor gone. She poured herself a shot of Jack Daniels and sat down to think. She decided to change her clothes first. She went into her bedroom, and while she was changing, she came across the piece of paper Aiden had given her. She stared at it and carried it with her to the living room.

Sipping her drink, she began to plan her course of action. The first thing to do was to contact a good lawyer. She knew Frank would help her. She decided that tonight she would just sleep. Tomorrow morning, she would decide what to do.

***

Luna woke up the next morning feeling rested. When she saw it was almost 10 o'clock, she jumped out of bed. While she was having her morning coffee, she called Frank and told him what had happened. Frank was sympathetic. He would help her get a good lawyer, no problem. He told her to take some leave, but Luna wanted to get to work. They would meet the following day.

With that settled, Luna sat down to work out her finances. Lawyers cost money, a lot of money. She checked her account to see how much she had. Suddenly, she remembered that she hadn't called her mother. She knew her mother would not approve of her decision to divorce her husband. Edna was old-fashioned. She decided to call her later with the news.

Then she fished out the piece of paper from Aiden and stared at it for a while. Should she call him? What would she say?

She decided to call, just to ask if he had reached home safely. Picking up her cell phone, she dialed the number. Aiden answered on the third ring.

She heard his familiar voice say, "Hello, who is this?"

"It's me, Luna."

"Hey Luna! Got home safely, I see," said Aiden.

"What about you? Did you get home safe?" Luna replied.

"When can we meet?" Aiden's voice came over the phone.

Luna was of two minds whether or not to tell him about what had just happened. She decided to tell him.

As she related the events, she could hear him softly cursing. But he didn't interrupt her.

Once she had finished, he said, "What's your address? I'm coming over to see you."

"No, that won't be necessary, Aiden. My boss is helping me with the lawyer and everything," she said.

"Listen, don't do anything until I get there. Your boss doesn't have the kind of lawyers I have on my payroll. I'm rich, remember?"

Luna laughed and gave Aiden her address.

"See you tomorrow!" he said, and disconnected the call. Luna sat staring at her phone.

Was that a clever decision, she wondered.

Chapter 12

Luna spent the day cleaning the house. She threw away the bedsheets that Marcus and the woman had used, ordered food online, and slept through the afternoon. Frank called later that evening and Luna invited him to come over.

He arrived looking worried. Luna told him to relax. Frank wanted to know if she was serious about divorcing Marcus, and she nodded.

"Okay, then. I'll call Allan tomorrow and set up an appointment for you," said Frank.

"No, Frank, not tomorrow. Give me a day or two to sort things out in my head," replied Luna.

"Let me take you out to dinner at least," Frank offered, and Luna accepted with alacrity. She didn't want to eat alone, not today.

During dinner, Luna and Frank talked about Luna's ordeal and her rescue. Frank was astonished at Aiden's capability. Luna's spirits revived and she chatted gaily. Frank was relieved that she had come out of her dark mood.

Returning to her apartment, Luna decided not to stress about the situation. What had needed to happen had happened. And that was all there was to it. She undressed and went to bed. She desperately wanted to see Sarah, but she was unable to make up her mind on what she would tell her daughter. That her father was not coming home? She slowly drifted off to sleep.

The next morning, Luna woke up at 6 am. She thought of going back to sleep again, but after tossing and turning for a few minutes, she decided to get up. After preparing a pot of strong coffee, she sat down to evaluate her position. Her marriage had broken down. She would have to raise Sarah as a single parent. That would have an impact on her job. Frank was understanding, but there were limits to how far even he could accommodate her need for time off. That worried her a great deal. She thought of bringing her mother over and asking her to stay and look after Luna. Marcus would try to get custody of Sarah, he had said so. That was a terrifying thought, and she needed to know if there was any chance of such a thing happening. She put her head in her hands and tried to shut out all her thoughts.

The phone rang, and when she picked it up, she saw that it was Aiden calling.

"I'm downstairs. Which floor are you on?" he asked.

"Sixth floor, apartment 6C," said Luna, getting up and going to the door. She felt a surge of excitement. Aiden was here!

He stepped out of the elevator, put his bag down on the ground, and took Luna in his arms. Luna didn't resist. She hung onto him.

She invited Aiden in, and he walked inside and looked around.

"Nice apartment," he said.

Luna asked him to sit down. As he did, she noticed that he was carrying the backpack. She smiled to herself.

"Have some coffee," she offered, pouring Aiden a cup.

They both sipped their coffee in silence. Aiden was staring at her, but Luna didn't feel uncomfortable. She realized she was not only relieved, but a tad happy. This man's mere presence gave her a sense of confidence.

Finally, Aiden put his cup down and said, "I knew there was trouble brewing between you and your husband, even though you denied it. I know you very well. As I said, you are not a very proficient liar. Now, tell me everything."

Luna told him about how she arrived home to find her husband in bed with some woman who looked like a tart, and probably was one.

Aiden listened in silence. But his face had grown hard. "Where is that bastard now?"

"I don't know. I threw him out immediately. He took some of his belongings and his tart and left," said Luna.

"Lucky for him that he did. " said Aiden.

Luna saw the menace on his face and felt apprehensive. This was the look of a man who was about to do something drastic.

"Calm down, Aiden," she warned, pouring him some more coffee.

"Where's your daughter? Still at your mother's?" he asked.

"Yes. I haven't told my mother yet," said Luna. She was desperate to see her daughter. But she comforted herself—Sarah was in safe hands. She needed this end sorted out first.

Then getting up and pacing the room," I need to see my daughter. Although she is happy with my mother, I really miss her. But I have to get my own head in order first."

"You have to tell her, you know," he said, and Luna nodded.

Aiden got up and began pacing around the room.

"What do you plan to do now? Divorce the guy, or what?" Aiden asked.

"Of course. I don't want him back in my life," replied Luna.

"Good. Now, about a lawyer. Have you hired one?" asked Aiden, sitting down at the table again.

"No, not yet. Frank is going to help me get one. He has a friend who is a divorce lawyer," Luna explained.

"Forget Frank. I'll get you one of the best lawyers there is for this kind of thing. He is handling my case," replied Aiden, pulling out his cell phone.

"Wait, wait," said Luna.

"For what?" asked Aiden, looking a little surprised.

"Your lawyer is certainly going to be expensive. Unlike you, I'm not rich, remember?" Luna reminded him with a laugh. She was already feeling better.

Aiden smiled. "You don't have to worry about paying him. He is on retainer with my company. The company account will pay him. Richie rich, remember?"

Luna tried to speak, but saw that Aiden already had the phone to his ear.

He said a few words and then disconnected the line. "He will handle it, no problem. I've asked him to come here. He will be here tonight."

Luna had the feeling that her life had just been taken over by Aiden.

She looked at the time and got up. "I have to go to the office!" she exclaimed.

"Tell your boss that you're busy and not coming in today. He'll understand. He knows what you have been through." said Aiden calmly.

"Yes. He gave me a week off, but I told him I would be in the office today," said Luna, a little defensively.

Still, Luna did as she was bid. She called Frank and excused herself for the day. Frank did not demur.

Aiden got up and looked out of the window. "How about some breakfast?" he suggested.

Luna went into the kitchen. She didn't know what was in the fridge; Marcus may have finished whatever was there. She found eggs and a packet of bacon.

Aiden ate with gusto. "Don't eat airline food. It's rubbish!" he said in between mouthfuls.

Luna watched him eat with a sense of satisfaction. She became aware of a sense of ease pervading her thoughts.

When he was done with breakfast, Aiden sat on the sofa and stretched out his legs. He called Luna over and asked her to sit beside him.

"Now, Luna, what are your plans for the future?" he asked, putting his arm around her.

"Honestly, Aiden, I don't know. Everything happened too quickly," she said, and nestled closer to him.

"Then I suggest you listen to me. I have a new house very close to my old one. I live there. My old house is occupied by my uncle. I want you to come with me and live there. The divorce will take time, but that's not a problem. The important thing is to take care of you," said Aiden, in a tone of what could only be love.

"Aiden, I need some time to decide," said Luna. "I have to think about my daughter."

"She can come and live with us. You seriously don't think I want you to leave your daughter somewhere? Besides, I don't have any children. Sarah will be my daughter."

Luna looked at his face and saw that he was really in dead earnest. "That's a nice thought, thank you," she said.

They sat there in silence, without moving. Luna was content.

After almost thirty minutes had passed, Aiden poked Luna and said, "Why don't you make some more coffee? It'll be like old times at the cabin!"

Luna got up and went to the kitchen. While she was making coffee, she heard Aiden talking on his cell phone.

They sat together and drank their coffee. Aiden kept looking at her, as if he was trying to say something.

"Your mother. She lives in the same house, near our old house?" he asked.

"No. We moved to a new house after your family fired my mother," said Luna.

"I see. Where's the new house?" he wanted to know.

"A little farther up the river to the north. She owns it now. She bought the place. Of course, I helped her with some money," said Luna.

"That means close to my new house! That's just great!" exclaimed Aiden.

Luna remained silent.

"Don't you see? Your mother! She can come and live with us, without leaving her own neighborhood. And Sarah can have her grandmother for company!" said Aiden in an excited tone.

Luna was a little taken aback at Aiden's enthusiasm. "I haven't told my mother yet. I don't know how she will react. Then, there is Sarah, my daughter. I have to consider her feelings, too. This isn't easy."

"No, it isn't, I know that," said Aiden. "But leave your mother to me. I'm very good at convincing people. I'm sure she will recognize me."

Luna looked at Aiden. "You seem to be taking over my life. Don't I get to decide anything?" she asked.

Aiden threw up his hands. "Of course, the final decision is yours. Just trying to help. It's going to be hard on everyone, especially Sarah."

Luna nodded. She knew it would be very difficult.

It was almost noon and Luna needed to cook lunch for two. But there wasn't much left in the fridge. She would have to order food.

Aiden had noticed her quick glance at her watch and then her thoughtful look.

"Don't worry about lunch. I know a very good gourmet joint here and the proprietor knows me well. I will order lunch. You're going to love the food," said Aiden.

Then he looked at Luna and added, "Hungry?"

"Not yet. I'll tell you when I am," she said.

"Well, the delivery will take time. At least an hour," said Aiden, pouring himself some more coffee.

"Why did you leave your old house?" she asked.

"After my parents passed away, I didn't want to live there. Dad had bought some land farther north, so I decided to build a house and move. My uncle lived in a small house, so I asked him to come live in the old house," explained Aiden.

He looked at her. "There is one thing you should know. I didn't know that my family fired your mother. I heard about it much later."

After this, they reminisced about old times. They had many beautiful memories to share.

They talked about the picnics in the woods, their secret meetings, and their thoughts on life. They realized how naive they had been. But Aiden was convinced that their plans were now bearing fruit. He seemed sure that Luna was going to marry him. Luna felt comfortable and it suddenly felt natural. She went along with him. She needed him now more than ever. The cabin experience had shown his resilience and capability.

When lunch arrived, the food was superb. She wanted to say that it was tasty, but thought that would be like saying the Mona Lisa was a nifty painting. Aiden sure knew his subject. What else did he know, Luna wondered.

After lunch, Aiden said, "Luna, you go nap in the bedroom. I'll settle here on the sofa. You need to have a clear head when Harry gets here."

"Harry?" asked Luna.

"My lawyer. He's a Brit, but a damned good lawyer. You'll see."

Luna went to her bedroom and stood for a while; she felt like an automaton. Resistance failed her. Should she ask Aiden to join her? She decided against it and lay down. Within minutes, she was fast asleep.

A knock on the bedroom door woke her. She slipped out of bed and opened the door to see Aiden grinning at her.

"Come on, sleepy head, come and have some coffee," he said, holding the door open for her.

"I'll be right there," she said.

While they sat drinking coffee, Luna remembered that she needed to speak to her mother before the lawyer came. She picked up her cell phone and, excusing herself, went to her bedroom and closed the door.

"Mamma, how are you?" she asked, and her mother replied that she was fine.

Sarah came on the line. "Mommy, when are you coming to get me?"

"Very soon, baby, very soon. Can you pass the phone to Grandma?"

Luna's mother came back on the line, and Luna told her what had happened. Her mother listened in silence, then said, "What are you going to do now?"

"I have an idea, Mamma. But I can't tell you just now. I will call you tomorrow. Give my love to Sarah. And Mamma, thank you for looking after her," said Luna, and disconnected.

She knew if she allowed her mother to offer suggestions and advice, the conversation would drag on for a long time. She didn't need that kind of thing right now.

Stepping into the living room, Luna saw Aiden laughing and talking to someone on his cell phone. When he saw her, he disconnected the line with a quick, "See you."

"Harry's on his way. He's bringing a bottle of excellent wine," said Aiden. "And dinner will be from the same restaurant."

Luna's fascination for Aiden was growing by the hour.

"Harry is extremely clever. Don't hide anything from him. Be frank with him and tell him exactly what you want. Got that?" Aiden added.

Luna knew that Aiden was acting for her. This man had taken over completely. Strangely enough, she felt happy. A sense of security pervaded her mind. It dawned on her that she wanted it to happen.

Harry arrived shortly thereafter. He was a tall man, with salt and pepper hair, who wore a very expensive three-piece suit. He had an expensive-looking slim briefcase in his hand. There was the hint of a very delicate cologne. Under his arm, Luna saw a bottle wrapped in some kind of fancy paper. The wine, she thought.

"Harry, this is Luna. Luna, this is Harry."

"Pleased to meet you, Luna," said Harry.

Once they were all seated, Harry opened his briefcase and withdrew a small notebook and a pen.

"Okay, Luna. Give me the facts," he said, opening the notebook.

Luna told him everything: her suspicions and the events that led to her husband leaving the house.

"The apartment is in your name?" he asked, addressing Luna.

"Yes."

"How much does your husband make per year?"

"I don't exactly know."

"Do you have any letters or photos that show him with any of the ladies?"

"No, I don't."

"What about children? Do you have any?"

"Yes. A daughter, Sarah."

"How old?"

"Six."

"And presumably you desire to keep custody of her?"

"Yes, of course I do. That's the most important thing."

Harry raised his hand. "Just getting the facts, Luna, just getting the facts." He lowered his hand and said, "And how much do you earn?"

Luna answered with a glance at Aiden, who sat impassively. "My husband has threatened to fight me for custody," she told Harry in an excited voice. "He won't get it, will he?"

Harry smiled. "Not a chance."

She sank back onto the sofa, relieved.

"And you plan to stay here and continue to work?" Harry asked.

Before Luna could answer, Aiden cut in. "Listen, Harry, we plan to go and stay at my house."

"We? Where do we get the 'we' from?" asked Harry, turning toward Aiden.

"Me, Luna, and her daughter. That's the 'we,'" said Aiden.

Harry began to laugh. "My friend, your divorce isn't finalized yet. And this one has not even started."

"Is there any law that prevents us from living together while our divorces go through?" asked Aiden.

Harry shook his head. He reached down and picked up the wine, which he had carefully placed by his side.

"Can we have some of this?" he asked, looking at Luna.

Luna did the honors while Aiden and Harry chatted.

She was happy with the way things were going. She felt a sense of security. She was looking forward to building a life with Aiden and marrying him when their respective divorces were finalized.

Harry took the wine glass and raised a toast. "Don't worry, Luna. We have a good case. You will get what you want."

"She had better, Harry," said Aiden with a laugh.

"I will prepare the papers and send them to you," said Harry. Changing the subject, he asked, "Where are we going for dinner? I'm beginning to feel a bit peckish."

Aiden laughed and said, "We're not going anywhere, old friend. I'm having dinner delivered from Paolo's."

"Ah! Paolo's!" said Harry.

While eating dinner, they spoke about other matters. Harry told them about a few unusual dicorce cases he had handled, and Luna and Aiden laughed at the foibles of men and women.

After dinner, Harry took his leave, reassuring Luna. Aiden and Luna were alone.

"Let me make some coffee," said Aiden, heading for the kitchen. Luna didn't have the strength to stop him. She just sat down.

Over coffee, Aiden asked Luna about what her mother had said.

"I just told her what happened. Not about my plans." said Luna. "I didn't have any plans at that moment, did I?" she added.

Aiden looked at her pensively. "No, you didn't."

"Aiden, are you sure we're doing the right thing? I mean, us just living together?" asked Luna.

Aiden considered the question for a few seconds. "We're both adults. We married the wrong people.

Now, we want to rebuild our lives. What's wrong with that?"

"I mean, both our divorces aren't through yet. Legally, I'm still married to Marcus."

"To hell with Marcus," said Aiden. "I'm going to change. I'll crash on the sofa and you sleep in your bedroom."

He stood and picked up his backpack, heading for the bathroom. Luna sat silently. She was trying desperately to make up her mind.

When Aiden returned, Luna saw that he was wearing a pair of grayish pyjamas and a crumpled T-shirt of indeterminate age. She laughed out aloud.

"What's funny?" asked Aiden.

"Nothing, nothing," said Luna, getting up.

She took Aiden by his arm and led him to her bedroom. There, she pushed him down on the bed and began to systematically disrobe him. Aiden watched in silence. She then undressed quickly and, without any warning, sat astride the reclining Aiden, facing him.

Aiden had a smile on his lips as he reached out and took both her breasts in his hands. Luna leaned forward and kissed him hard while Aiden continued to fondle her breasts. She realized that he was giving her the lead role. But Luna knew how to play it. She took his penis in her hands and guided it inside her, and she began to move back and forth in a sliding motion. Aiden gasped for air. Luna started moving faster, chasing her own pleasure. As they climaxed, Luna leaned forward and slumped onto Aiden's chest. It was the same overwhelming passion she had experienced at the cabin.

Afterward, as she lay sated, the last fleeting thought that went through her mind before sleep overtook her was, "What is Mamma going to say?"